When
LOVE
Happens...

MANISH KUMAR

Srishti
PUBLISHERS & DISTRIBUTORS

SRISHTI PUBLISHERS & DISTRIBUTORS
Registered Office: N-16, C.R. Park
New Delhi – 110 019

Corporate Office: 212A, Peacock Lane
Shahpur Jat, New Delhi – 110 049
editorial@srishtipublishers.com

First published by
Srishti Publishers & Distributors in 2018

Dedicated to
"Me and You"

"I love you" – the three words that create emotions and joy in relationships. A statement formed with these words sounds lovely, but the story behind it and its aftermath is quite rational. They have their own value.

The first word "I" is most important initially, but after some time, "you" (for whom you are showing your emotions) takes priority. To keep the balance of "I" and "You" intact, one should know the real meaning of love.

Somewhere in this story, I wandered. But it's love that connected me with god and made me realize that self-worth is more important. That "I" has to come first.

I have tried to put in words a story which was already written years ago, but was confined in my heart till now.

Acknowledgements

I would like to thank everyone who played an important role in my life and made me so comfortable that I could think of writing a book.

Special thanks to my parents for their endless support, and for believing that I could make this possible.

A big thank you to team Srishti Publishers for believing in my manuscript, giving it a proper shape, and converting it into a book that could reach the readers.

Last, but not the least, thanks to myself for working so patiently over the past few years to give a final touch to this story. :)

Thanks to you as well, dear friends and readers, for reaching out to words I have written. Hope you will enjoy it with the same spirit with which I have written this book.

Note from the author

This book is based on some real life experiences but is a work of fiction. All names presented are fictitious to protect real identities.

Sometime in our lives, we feel too desolate, wishing that something could hold us, keep us engaged and give us courage to fight sadness. Nobody could do it better for me than my writing. Yes, this book.

I started writing with a faith that gave my fabulous soul some relief in the void my heart had created. However, it was nothing less than a wonder after having gone through so much trouble.

Being in love, I never thought of doing any wrong to anyone. The reason was my faith in god and hence the belief in myself, that everything would be fine. I knew believing in god would lead me towards coming face to face with my strength, and help in knowing the real me.

Different experiences in my life were the real lessons. Overall, a message delegated through this book is that true relationships or love do not mean that we restrict ourselves to questions and expectations. It is about exploring love and knowing its true value in a way that you can find yourself in a new delighted world.

Prologue

Teri har koshish wo dekh raha
Baitha upar aasmano mein...
Tu zor laga ud ja phir se,
Teri shakti hai tere armano mein...
Yun bandha nahi tu reh sakata,
Koi baandh tujhe nahi rakh sakta...

[He is watching over your struggles from above... Try harder and fly again, for your dreams are your strength. You cannot be shackled... nobody can tie you down.]

Koi farishta tujhe chhudayega,
Jo aayega aasmano se...
Bas pankh phaila tu zor laga,
Teri pehchan hai teri udano se.
Tere raaste hain asmano mein,
Tere rishte hain asmano se.
Tu zor laga ek aur laga...

[Angels will fly down from the sky and set you free. Spread your wings and try, your identity is in your flight. Your path

is in the sky, for you have a relationship with the sky. Try
yet again, try magnificently, just one more time…]

An eagle was stuck between the branches of a tall tree. It was
fluttering its wings, trying in vain to free itself. I was in Bangalore,
far away from my home in Bihar and about to enter my office
building, when I noticed the unhappy eagle. I had my usual long,
hard day of work ahead of me. But I stood there, letting the minutes
tick away, as I contemplated on how to rescue the bird. I knew how
to scale the tallest, most dangerous of telecom towers, but I had
no idea of how to climb a gigantic tree. For some reason, it had
become very important for me to see that the eagle was safe and
could fly again. So I stayed there, stopping the odd interested person
and asking them if they had any idea to help the big, beautiful
bird. While there were many sympathetic people, no one could do
anything to help.

As I stood there, engrossed in the plight of the bird, my manager
came by. As expected, he shouted at me for wasting time when
there was so much work to be done. He couldn't care about the
eagle suffering, or anyone else for that matter. He had contracts
and obligations to fulfill and we were the engineers responsible for
doing it.

I was working for a sub-vendor company that handled projects
for vendors (provide equipment) who in turn had contracts with
telephone companies (provide services to users for communication
or internet) to provide the infrastructure required for their service
networks. There was a lot of competition amongst the sub-vendors
as contracts were based on cost and time. The criteria for selection
of sub-vendors were:

> 'who could work 24/7, who will finish first, who has the largest
> number of worker bees… oops… employees and who are the
> cheapest.'

Graduate degrees, college scores or talent were the least of their concerns. Once these sub-vendors secured a contract, the war was on to finish the project. Nobody cared how it was done.

The only way to be both cost-effective and time-effective was to provide the bare minimum in terms of wages and days off, to the actual workers working on creating the network. I was one such worker, had been for a while, and was desperate to get out of the industry, like the trapped eagle.

In my job, eagles were a nuisance. In some places, they nested on the mobile towers, and attacked us when we tried to go up there to do our work. But here, it was injured and in agony and I could not help but feel sorry for it. Suddenly, I was more irritated than ever with my job, where there was no room for kindness and compassion or even time for a personal life. I wanted to get out but hadn't yet found a way to do so.

The eagle's family was trying to help him. They fed him bits of food but could do nothing to free him. I left the place to finish my assignments for the day but kept wondering about the fate of the bird. As I left the place, I prayed to god to save the bird. Similarly, every day, I pleaded with god to help me find a way out of this situation I had gotten myself into. Having shelled out thirty thousand for the training and having depended on my family for a very long time, I was in no position to let go of this job without finding another.

When I got back to the office that night, I anxiously looked up at the tree. The bird was gone! I asked around and found out that finally some people had been able to go up there, break the branches and release the bird. Suddenly, it struck me… it is good to keep trying to get out of a bad situation, even if it seems as though you cannot come out of it completely. This was the first time I had seen a helpless eagle. But, it did not sit in silence, tolerating his miserable position. It made noises, drew attention to its struggles and tried hard to get out of the situation. And, someone, somewhere responded to his efforts and helped release him. Thank you god!

The next day, I was traveling in the office cab to reach my work spot, where I was supposed to work on a tower. It was quite a distance away from Bangalore. Sitting in the back seat of the cab, I stared at the barren summer landscape outside. I was sweating inside the hot cab and drinking boiled water to cool myself when once again, I remembered the eagle. The eagle was able to escape, I thought. God never disappoints! Suddenly, I was transported back in time to a day in my childhood when my prayers had been answered promptly…

Early Impressions

A chunk of hard earth hit my head. I had tried my best to convince the opposing team that they had violated the rules of the game. However, they were unwilling to listen to me and wanted to declare themselves the winners. I was twelve years old, amongst a group of boys of similar age from my village, and we were playing football. I was injured but my teammates were too busy throwing stones at the opposing team to pay any attention to me.

The wound was not too deep, but after I touched the injured spot on my head, I found blood on my fingers. But my real problem was not my injury or loss of blood, it was my parents. I lived in the village of Biharsharif, eighty kilometres from Patna, where lie the ruins of the ancient Nalanda University. Farming and agriculture is the chief source of income in this part of the state and my family too owned some land here. Although my parents were college graduates, they chose to remain in their native village and farm their land. But, they were strict about our education and we were expected to do well in school.

I was at an age when parents tend to blame our mischievousness for every misfortune that befalls us. So naturally, I was scared that I would be punished for going home with blood on my head and began to pray to god to spare me a beating. There is a big Shiva temple near my village. The top of the dome is visible from the playground. I turned towards the temple and implored, please save me Bhole Nath! Then I picked up some soil and rubbed it in and this stopped the little trickle of blood coming out of the wound. Before entering my house, I took the towel that we usually carried around with us while going out to the fields and twisted it around my head like a turban. My parents did not comment on it that night or the next morning. But when I did the same thing the next evening too, they realized that something was wrong.

My mother came up to me, touched the makeshift turban and asked, "Why are you wearing it?" And then, she removed the turban from my head.

I was scared and tried to justify it in the best way I could. I looked at my mother's face to read her expression. But her face did not reveal anything. She looked calm, as usual. And when she went away without saying anything, I was very surprised. I looked in the mirror and saw that the wound was not visible any longer. You saved me Bhole Nath! My faith in god was strengthened.

Our life is more or less based on our childhood impressions; what we do, what we wish to do, our enjoyments and our disappointments are all reflections of our childhood experiences. So make your childhood good for a better adult life.

Fear of loss is one of the chief reasons behind human worries. But, what kind of fear can there possibly be during childhood? Hope starts at an early age and carries on until our first experience of loss. This can either make a negative impression on us or even be the beginning of something positive. A lot of thinking and positivity would be required to ensure that our experiences leave encouraging impressions on us.

We were small-time farmers and despite college degrees, hardly anybody in the family had any jobs. It was not easy to meet all our needs and educate the children on an annual income of less than thirty thousand rupees. Most of the income from farming would be recycled back into the farm due to crop losses, rain failure or numerous other reasons. For us, agriculture was pretty much like gambling, there was no guarantee that we would even get back the money invested in it, forget making a profit!

I was good in mathematics and had a lot of interest in science since childhood, but it was hard to do anything much about it because of the lack of a guide and mentor. However, there was one person, an uncle in the neighborhood, who had an engineering degree from IIT. His family background was similar to mine but with a slightly better financial condition. He became my inspiration to aim for an improved life. I thought, if he could become an engineer, why couldn't I become one as well? If his background hadn't stopped him from achieving his goals, why should my background, which is similar to his, stop me? For me, getting into an engineering college and specifically into one of the IITs became a mission. It was a way to break generations of financial difficulties and become successful in my own right.

I was mild-mannered and would trustfully make friends with even unknown people. I felt good when I loved and helped people unconditionally. Some people said it was naiveté, some said I was foolish, but I did not care and did what I felt was right. My parents had always made sure to teach me right from wrong and instilled the belief that as long as I did my part, worked honestly and respectfully and trusted god, I would be successful. So, it was only natural for me to fall in love with someone.

It became more joyful when that friend was my classmate since the last four years and became very special with every passing day. Slowly, something pulled our attention towards each other. We'd engage in little conversations without words – something naughty I'd do would make her smile, and she would bend her head smiling and keep her fingers on her lips, or a cute slap gesture to which I would forward my cheek from a distance.

She was this beautiful girl in my town who was the epitome of all the qualities that I valued the most: simplicity, generosity and willingness to help others.

I had known her since childhood and called her 'G' as I saw god in her big, brown and innocent eyes. Or at least, that is how I felt because I had a lot of respect for her. However, we hardly spoke to each other as we lived in a conservative little town. Interaction between boys and girls was traditionally not encouraged and we did not speak much to the girls in our school. The girls too were scared of causing unnecessary rumours and followed the restrictions imposed on them by culture, tradition, family and society.

When I was in the twelfth standard, in the classroom, there was a two-row seating arrangement, separately for boys and girls. Very few of us carried school bags to carry our notebooks or books. Instead, we happily carried one or two notebooks or books for the lecture classes of the day. It was the new millennium, late 2001. We all were young at heart and modern in school, no matter how old tradition, society or the sciences were. Our school days were the most wonderful days; there was nothing to look back on and also there was no fear about the future. We purely lived in the present.

♋

After a long wait of three years, we were all grown up in our eyes. I worked up the courage to write to G to confess my feelings for her. I wrote a few words on a piece of paper:

Please reply if you love me. I trust you are also in love with me… sorry for the brief note. Once I'm sure, we can have more detailed communication.

It was a secret between us. Sometimes, she would laugh and gesture in my direction, which made me a little confident that she liked me as well. I had no intention of hurting her, but I knew I would definitely be hurt if she were to deny any sort of feelings towards me. And, I did not want anyone else hearing about this. So I even made sure to include,

If you are not interested in me, please don't disclose this to anyone else.

And thus began our journey towards the unknown, without any thoughts of plans for the future.

I was surprised but happy to get the following reply –

Tumne itni si baat ke liye itna time laga diya. Took you four years to confess.

I have been expecting this from you for a long time now. I love you, I like you, I want you...

She sent her note to me in the same way that I had passed along the note to her – hidden inside the outer wrapper of a book. For a long time, we communicated with each other in this way, without anyone's knowledge.

What kind of joy it was to be in a relationship, not sharing it with anyone but the two of us, and a happiness which tickled the soul. Our heads bent only to hide the smiles of affection, and a smile rose to look up in the sky to share the feelings and joy with nature, wondering how marvelous a heart feels in love.

It is said that love is blind, but in our case, it was deaf and dumb as well, as we could only write to each other. No dating, no talking to each other or even looking at each other, as someone could catch us staring and then it would be a problem for her. A conditional love proposal – *No one should be aware of our relationship* – she was very strict about this. Sometimes, we wouldn't be able to see each other or communicate with each other for long periods of time, but there was nothing I could do about it. This kind of love I handed over to god. I could not quit as I was very serious about it and considered it true love. She was more concerned about her family and the scandal the revelation of our relationship could cause; being a girl, tradition and reputation were more important for her. For me, *love* were more important. It was true love (at least I felt love and later realized it was true) and I wanted to make sure that it would last forever.

Her friend helped us pass the books with our letters to each other. G did not want to do it directly as she was scared. She was a timid girl. Her friend was bolder and kind enough to help us. We tried to think of other safer ways of exchanging letters, but we both couldn't think of anything.

Once G had to pass on an urgent message to me while we all were in the classroom; she, her friends, two of my friends and I were all standing at different positions but I was standing near my desk and G's friend was standing near me, holding a stick. I was not aware of what was going on and was not able to see her stick as I was concentrating on a face (G's of course!).

Suddenly one of my friends pulled out something from my book and ran way. It was only after a minute that I realized what had happened. I followed him and after a long chase, I caught him and asked, "Give me whatever you are holding."

I was sure it was a letter given by her and if someone found out, I shuddered thinking of the consequences. G's friend had been pointing her stick towards my book, but I had been too busy looking at G's face.

After much pleading, my friend finally agreed to give it to me but said gasping, "I will not disclose this to anybody… please let me read the letter first."

I agreed as I thought he wouldn't give it to me otherwise.

When I returned to the classroom, there were a lot of questions from G and her friend. G was tensed. "What were you thinking, you stupid boy?" she uttered.

I was blushing but was scared too and with a shy face I said I was sorry. I was happy because this was the first time she had spoken to me, albeit angrily. I was also a little scared as she was angry and worried that people would hear us. I did not care about myself, but did not want to offend her. I just wanted to win her trust, no matter what.

♋

As days passed, a negative thought kept troubling me. What if she rejects me in the future? I wanted to know how much she loved me and wondered how to go about it.

At dusk, I would go to my friend's house five kilometres away from my house. He was her neighbour. I would watch her in her garden and on her roof. She would also notice me watching her. This continued for a few months. I only always watched her, but did not approach her in any way. We continued to exchange letters but I had wondered how long we would continue like this. Why couldn't we talk for a few minutes? Doesn't she want to meet me?

I was surprised when one day a child came and told me with a smile, "G is calling you near her house." I was nervous, shocked, surprised. My palms and soles became cold as nothing like this had happened before. It was happening now, when I really wanted it to.

What happened? Why did she call me? What will she ask? Has somebody found out about us? A lot of questions came up in my mind. I asked my friend whether I should go and he said that I should, only if to see what happens. When I reached the spot near her garden, she was not there yet. I had to wait for a few minutes, curiosity clubbed with nervousness clouded my mind. Finally I saw her coming out from her house. She was wearing a yellow salwar-suit with a red dupatta. The sound of her footwear echoed in my ear. She reached up to me. I was hardly able to look at her face or make eye contact, but I still remember her grey footwear. She came near me adjusting her dupatta from one shoulder to the other. I felt shy.

I began to look in the opposite direction. She walked up to me smiling and asked, "What are you looking at?"

"Umm... nothing!" Looking up from the corner of my eye for a moment, I replied shyly.

"Then, look at me and talk," she said.

She smiled as I blushed.

Then she said surprisingly, "Give me a book and I will return it to you after some days."

I was confused and stammered, "Book... which book?"

"Budhu! Any book," she replied with a big smile.

I stood wondering why she needed a book from me.

She said shaking her head, "Give me *Concept of Physics, Part I.*"

I said with a smile when I realized what she was trying to do, "Oh... got it! Sure, you will get it."

The child who had been the messenger was standing there but was not mature enough to understand what was going on. Although this was the first time she had called me to talk to her for a few minutes, there was nothing to talk about.

After that day, I continued to sit on my friend's roof, waiting for her to notice me. There was a cowshed in front of her house and their servants fed the cows and oxen everyday. One day, G's uncle came to feed the cattle instead. I felt a little disturbed but I sat there as usual. The roof of the house was visible from the cowshed and her uncle could see me. Her uncle was feeding the cattle and one of them was shaking its head and ears whenever he tried to feed it. The third time it did that, he turned into an angry young man and shouted,

"Doonga kaan ke niche… saara joonoon sar se niche aa jayega."

[Will give you a blow and all your passion and arrogance will vanish.]

He was shouting at the cow, but staring directly at me. My heart pounded. I was completely jellified, frozen and very scared. I thought I should move, but could not make myself to get up. I strongly felt that his words were directed towards me, especially as the cattle were completely calm and standing on the other side of the shed. I wondered if someone had revealed the matter to him or if he had watched us and guessed what was going on. What will happen now? I wondered. Meanwhile, she came out onto the roof, laughing, but I was scared and a number of thoughts were running around in my head. By this time, her uncle had gone inside and I wondered if she had seen this little incident. I felt sure she must have seen it and was enjoying it, especially because she must have seen my face and realized how scared I was. On the other hand, when I saw her laughing, I thought we must be safe. She was happy, so that meant nobody in her home knew about us. If they did, she would have asked me to forget it and end the relationship. I was becoming more serious day by day and worried as well, because there was no indication about the future of our relationship.

I don't know how to describe her in words; she had a fair face with a black mole near her left eye and curly hair, half of which she'd keep in front over her right shoulder. She had beautiful innocent eyes. For me, she was simply a girl in whose eyes I saw god. She was G and initially I was very happy. There was no dilemma in my mind when I loved her in silence. But, once she said yes, I began to go through a gamut of mixed emotions, ranging from love and excitement to fear and negativity. I was scared she might suddenly come to me and tell me that she wanted to end it because of problems with her family as she was very scared of society. This changed me completely.

I was seriously in love and wanted to share it with my friends, who were aware of it. They made fun saying this was 'time pass' love and even though I did not mind their comments visibly, on the inside, I wondered about true love and innocence. I knew that she loved me, but I wondered if she was sure about her own feelings. It was very difficult for me to judge all this through our written communication as it was both little and delayed. I couldn't get an immediate response as most of the time we had to wait a while to find a favourable opportunity to exchange letters. Slowly I realized that she was worried about her family; she was scared of her father and about what he would do if he found out. The family's reputation was on her mind.

∽

She came from a rather well-known family in the village, but I was from a simple one. Now, our friends were aware of this situation but our families did not know anything about it. We continued to write and pass messages for a long time, but once she sent a written note asking,

How long will we continue to write and communicate? Do you not want to meet me?

I read this message and got emotional. I wanted to meet her too, but how would we be able to? What if someone saw us? It was difficult for her to even get out of her house; she could not go anywhere except to her neighbour's place. I was also worried about what would happen to me in the future. Then after some days, she sent another note.

As of now we will stop communication through letters, but later I will guide you about how we can meet.

I was taken aback with this vague note. She had asked me to stop writing but at the same time I thought she must be excited about our meeting. We were seeing each other every day in school but there was no reaction on her face, things continued like this for five to six months and I continued to worry. I asked her friends and my friends to find out what the story was, but there was no response. My days in the twelfth standard were about to end. Five more months were left and after that it would be very difficult to even see each other. I tried to explain all this and get some response from her, but without any success. I felt suffocated in my heart in an indescribable way, but couldn't do anything; nor was there anybody to help me.

One of my best friends was Amar, who was her neighbour and good friend, and was on good terms with her family as well.

Amar could be trusted by G and I was thankful for his presence. He could be trusted with our secret.

Amar came to me and said, "I have a surprise for you."

I said, "What?"

He told me, "I do not want anything from you but just let me read this, that's all!"

I was happy that she had written to me after a long time. I told him that I wanted to read it first and then I would give it to him. When I read it I was completely shattered for the first few moments. This was the first time I was experiencing heartbreak. I was down on my knees, teary-eyed.

Amar asked me, "What happened?"

When I did not respond, he took the paper from my hand, read it and said, "Sorry, I was not aware about this. I thought it was good news for you."

Then he said distraught, "I told you earlier also, do not be so serious regarding this matter, one day you'll get hurt."

I said, blinking my eyes, "I had really not expected my heart to hurt me so much."

The letter was written in Hindi,

Har insan ke paas ek dil hota hai aur wo dil main kisi aur ko de chuki hun, mujhe maaf kar do, woh yahan ka nahi hai

[Everybody has one heart and that heart I have given to someone else. Please excuse me, he is not from this place.]

When I read it, I had a doubt that this may not be true. I felt she was hiding something from me.

I was agitated and replied in a single line,

I will never be back in your life again.

I realized she must be afraid of her family so had made up this excuse to break up. But how would I know and there was nothing I could do.

One thing was clear that she was a timid and thoughtful girl who worried about family, respect, honour and so on. I believed in those as well, but why did she have to take such a step, I wondered. Did she think that I wouldn't be able to support her and give her whatever she wanted? Or did she think because I was from a simple family, I didn't have any respect in society? I don't know but she had always said, "You don't know my family. They are very strict. If they find out about this, they will kill me first." When she told me this, I thought, why should I do something that could get someone killed?

I was saddened and lost when I heard that she loved someone else. It was hard to rid my mind of her memories. On the other hand, I also had doubts about what she had written. Questions ran amok in my mind. I could not figure out how to find the answers.

I felt totally dependent on god and left my questions to him. Sometimes I would think that it was all just a daydream. Love is cold as ice but at the same time, it is a hot fireball too. My heart experienced things that are tough to explain even today.

She was always on my mind and in my heart and I had a tough time for five or six years.

I was sad and constantly unhappy with thoughts of G teasing my mind, and had no idea how to get help.

Luckily I met Asha after a long time. She used to guide me since my childhood on all matters. A good friend, she was older than me and had a job too. After meeting me, she sensed from my expression that something was wrong and asked me to stop pretending. "You look like a worried man. Is something wrong? I know you are trying to be cheerful."

Surprisingly, I answered with a half-smile on a sad face. "Nothing," I said, as I wanted to hide my real state from her. But she was quite excited and wanted to know more. She saw my sadness and said she was sure there was a girl involved and insisted that I tell her everything. I was suddenly scared she may figure everything out and reveal it to my parents. I was trying to think of something to tell her and come up with some excuses when she told me not to worry, that she wouldn't disclose my problems to anybody.

"Tell me in detail who it is, and what the problem is. I will try my best to get you both together," she pressed.

I would get some relief from my pain if I shared it with someone, but I did not want this matter to reach my parents. They had great expectations from me and this was an age to focus on studies. I did not want to make them unhappy. Asha continued to assure me that she would guide us and show us the right path. In good faith, I described the whole story to her. She was in a state of wonder and said excitedly, "I know this girl. If you want to give her a letter, I can pass it on to her."

I requested her hesitatingly if she could help us meet as we had only written to each other over the last few years and had never had a chance to meet and talk to discuss our issue. She agreed to talk to G and arrange for her to meet me.

After a few days, when Asha met G, she asked her about me and why she had pushed me away. G was surprised that Asha knew our story and was annoyed that I was telling people about it. Asha calmed her and reassured her that she would keep our secret. After gathering some courage, G revealed the truth; she had done so because her family had begun to suspect her and she wanted to prevent any further problems. Asha asked her why she couldn't have just told me the truth. She said that she thought it was the best way to prevent me from trying to contact her again.

Asha realized that G may still love me so she decided to set up the meeting. G's older sister was getting married, so Asha told G that it would be the perfect occasion to meet me and talk. G refused saying that it was risky and someone might catch us.

The next day Asha asked me to meet her near her office. She took me to the canteen and told me about her meeting with G over a cup of tea. She didn't look excited so I knew there wasn't good news. She told me how afraid G was about her family finding out and how she had refused to meet me.

"You are sensible, so now you can understand yourself that if someone can so easily give up on you, then it is time for you to move on as well."

She walked me to the office gate, "If you are no longer important to someone, make yourself precious in your view. Let go."

I was shattered and began to walk towards a lonely place, near a tank (definitely not to drown myself), sat for a few minutes, gathered myself and then began talking to god, questioning him as to why I was made to suffer. The tears would not stop flowing. Amar happened to walk by and was surprised to see me in such a state. He quietly rubbed my back and tried to cheer me up by saying that there were other girls in the world and I should just forget G. I embraced him and cried bitterly.

Childhood is a time for fun, curiosity, enjoyment and happiness, but in my case, it was the opposite. It felt like a curse that I could not make sense of. Maybe for others losing their first love would be a normal part of growing up, but for me, it was truly heartbreaking.

My schooling was almost over; I was about to complete my twelfth standard. Now I had to decide what I wanted to study further. Although my family's financial resources were modest, they were ready to pay for my higher education. I had decided that I wanted to study engineering. But my broken relationship hindered me from focusing on my career goals. As the days went by, the situation became more serious but my parents had no idea about it.

One day Asha asked me to meet her as she was going out of station for a few months. She wanted to see me before she left.

When I did, in her courtyard garden, she sensed the same worry on my face.

"So she is still on your mind? We cannot see what is in G's heart, how she feels about you, what kind of notion she has about love… but if you continue this one-sided love of yours, you will be permanently unhappy," she chided me.

"Why did she play with my feelings?" I responded in a sad, unsteady voice. "She could have directly told me about her problem. I think she did this for fun and now that our schooling is over, she is not interested in me anymore. Okay, let it be… God bless her! I am happy."

Asha sighed, "Now you stop thinking about her. You have your future, so you think about yourself, not about her. She will get married and leave, but you will be wasted. So, first take care of yourself. You want her and even if she wants you, there is no real possibility of you both getting married."

I controlled my emotions and told her that I was fine and would focus on doing better for myself.

Placing a hand around my shoulder, Asha exclaimed happily, "Good boy! She said rubbing my shoulders as I silently sobbed, "Calm down, control yourself."

I requested Asha to return all of G's letters to G and she did it for me. G said that I was misunderstanding her, but I had made up my mind. I would focus on what was important. I had been a good student, was strong in my fundamentals and was confident of crossing any hurdles in academics. But true love always has memories and when that love is broken, it results in an aching heart and mind. I could not forget all that had happened and decided that I would excel career-wise and would show her what I was. My success would be like sweet revenge. But that, as I was soon to learn, was easier said than done.

♋

It was time to move out of my native town to a place where I could earn as well as prepare myself for better education. I decided to prepare for the engineering entrance exams rather than take admission in any graduate stream.

I rented a tiny room in Patna for around three hundred rupees per month. It was box-like and dark and one had to bend to get through the door.

It was the first time that I was living away from my family and I struggled. Thankfully, my cousin who lived in the city was of great help. My dream was to get into an IIT to pursue my education in engineering and I wanted to make sure that the dream would come true.

"Candidates should be single-minded in their aim." An IITian first rank holder had once said this in a magazine interview.

However, my heart and mind were elsewhere, no matter how hard I tried to focus. Despite fighting against it, it became more important for me to find and regain the love that I had lost. Half my mind was on love and the other half on my studies, so I wasn't making any progress. Moreover, English was very important to be able to get into the IITs. Coaching classes for specific subjects were helpful, but English was a problem for me. I was a student educated in the Hindi medium and it took me a long time to pick the required English language skills. Due to all these hurdles, I was not able to get into any of the IITs in the first few attempts.

Slowly, due to overthinking, emotional stress and work, I began to suffer from headaches. If the heart has a problem, the mind can help, if the mind has a problem, the heart can help, but if both have problems, who will help? I decided to go to a doctor.

I had gone to the doctor because of my frequent headaches. After seeing him and buying my medicines, I went back to my room. My landlord told me that a girl had called for me while I was out and she had stated that she was my sister. Those were the days before mobile phones. I did not have a landline in my room, but had given my landlord's number to my family and friends. Later on, I heard from my friend Amar that G had called me. She had met Amar in the market and had asked for my number.

That night, I was once again missing G and feeling very sad. Why did she call me? She had broken up, after all. Did she still love me? My mind was full of questions. It was midnight and I still hadn't been able to go to sleep. Whenever I would think about the past, tears would automatically start flowing from my eyes. In a sad coincidence, Kishore Kumar's *Mere naina sawan badho* was playing on my radio. Inevitably, I started sobbing loudly and could not control myself. At that moment, someone knocked on my door. I was completely confounded, and began to panic as I did not want anyone to see me in this state. I wiped my tears, took a few seconds to pull myself together, prepared myself to act cheerful, increased the volume of the radio and opened the door. My friend and neighbour Ashok stood outside.

He asked me, "What happened? I heard noises of crying from this room."

My face was sad and dull but I kept smiling. "Nobody was crying here," I told him in a cheerful voice ."It must have been the child next door."

I then went back to turn off the radio and pretended to listen. "No, the child is not crying anymore," I said.

Ashok did not buy it. He asked me directly, "Tell me, were you crying?"

I did not know what to say. He was my friend but at that time, I did not want to share this matter with him or anybody. What was the point? He would console me and even give suggestions about what I could do to cope with my sorrow, but none of that would really change things for me. Tomorrow, I would do the same thing. If I had really been able to forget it easily, I would not be writing this today. So, I usually did what my heart wanted me to do and the rest, I would leave to Lord Shiva.

It was a long story to tell someone who always thought I was a happy guy, so I continued to deny that I had been crying, with a fake smile. Luckily, Ashok was finally convinced that a child in the next room had been crying and he left without pestering me anymore about it.

Jisne bahaya ansuon ko
Wo kya jaane gam ka paimana…
Jisne piya hai ansuon ko
Wo hi jaane gam ka thikana.
Beh gaye ansu jo tere samjho kam hua tera gam
Jisne piya hai ise, uska badha ranjo gam.

Ansuon se shayad gam dikh jate hain
Unka kya jo ansuon ko pee jate hain!

[Those who weep freely, what do they know about sorrow?
The depth of human anguish is theirs, who refuse to weep.
Hot tears flow freely, your grief goes out of you. Crying
unveils sorrow; brings forth compassion. But what about
those who hold back and supress their tears?]

♋

Amar used to visit me frequently in Patna. When I met Amar again,
I asked him, "Do you have any idea how much she wants me or
how deep her love for me is? After all, you see her often when she
goes about her activities."

"Not sure yaar," Amar replied. "Her heart is something I cannot
see, and cannot say how much her heart is beating for you."

"Very funny!" I replied, annoyed and a little disappointed.
Sounded to me like she was happy and not pining for me, otherwise
Amar would have seen some difference in her behaviour. That is
okay, I thought, I want her to be happy. May god keep her smiling
always, I wished.

I usually went home to see my parents and family once or
twice a year. Like every other year, that year too in March 2003
I went home to celebrate Holi with my family. It was almost the
end of my third year in Patna. As usual, Amar came to celebrate and
meet me at home. After a while, he gave me a folded piece of paper.
I opened it and saw G's handwriting,

*Please write something and give it to me. I mean how are you, how do
you feel about me now? What do you think about me?*

Basically, she wanted to know if I still loved her or not. I did
not bother to reply to her note.

When I had come home, my family was always happy to see me, especially my mother. By then, it had been almost three-and-a-half years since I had left home. My mother, being sharp as all mothers, sensed that there was something bothering me. She could see it on my face.

"What happened?" she would ask me. "Are you all right, any difficulties in your studies?"

"I am fine Ma." I would try to convince her a number of times, coming up with some excuses. She would try to get me to talk to her, saying that no matter what the problem was, she would help me find a solution. When she would say such things, it would be hard for me to not break down and tell her everything. But I did not. I continued to convince her that I was doing well. Soon I returned to my studies. Even though I loved going home for visits, it was also a relief to get back to Patna. At least there, I could be myself without having to always pretend that I was happy. However, I was also learning to make myself happy.

♋

It had been a long time since I had left home for Patna in an effort to prepare and get into an engineering college of my choice. I still hadn't been able to do it. I was losing hope. It was completely my fault as my parents had encouraged and helped me all along, but I hadn't been able to reach my goal. It was hard for them to keep spending money on me so it was up to me now to understand their position and do something to support myself. I had to get into a college or continue preparing without their support. I decided to give it my best shot.

I had an important entrance exam coming up in the same city. The day before the exam, I thought I should go to the exam centre and confirm that it was the right place. I did not want to go there for the first time in the morning of the exam and face any unpleasant surprises. I had a bicycle to go for tuitions and coaching classes. Even though it looked like it would rain, I decided to cycle all the way there and check out the place. I reached the place and saw a staff member sitting at a table inside the office.

"Excuse me, sir," I said pleasantly. "My admit card says that this is the place for the engineering entrance exam tomorrow. I just want to confirm. Is this the right place?"

"Why should I confirm? Are you from the CBI? Just go away!" he replied, quite rudely.

I was shocked by his response.

"Sir, my place is quite far off from here and that is why I wanted to confirm," I stated quietly.

"Oh, just get out of here!" he shouted. "Stupid boys," he murmured.

I left the place, feeling nervous. It had started raining by then, so I started walking, rolling the bicycle along with me. I was unhappy with the way the man had spoken to me. Why did he talk to me like that, I wondered. And why was I not able to respond to him in the same manner?

My room was on the ground floor of an old building. So during heavy rains, my room would inevitably get flooded. The water came up to my knees but luckily my bed was above the water level and still dry.

I was still thinking of what had happened at the exam centre and feared that if I missed the exam the next day or didn't perform well, I would have to struggle for another long year.

That night, I managed to get some sleep in my water-logged room, erasing the events of the day. I could not think of anything else other than the exam. I was a little confident about this particular entrance test but there was some fear in my mind too. What will I do if I don't get through? The next morning I reached the exam hall on time and found the same man from the past day in the classroom as the invigilator. He saw me and it seemed as if he wanted to say something, but I turned away and took my seat. At the end of the exam, when I handed over my answer sheet to him, he smiled at me.

"Thanks sir," I said gleefully with a smile. He smiled to apologize and I smiled to forgive – two smiles from the heart for the truth. I told him quite confidently, "This will be my last exam. I won't have to appear for another entrance exam. I will get through this and get admission into an engineering college this year." The man smiled and wished me good luck.

"Thank you sir," I replied smiling. What a lesson learnt from this incident! No need to react; just sit back and wait. Those who are rude to you will eventually realize it themselves.

All this time, I had still not forgotten G. In conversation with Amar, I got updates of G but knowingly tried not to ask too much. However, another friend, a mischievous guy who had somehow found out about G and me, told G and her friend that I had drunk a small bottle of Dettol. He wanted to see what G's reaction would be as that would reveal her true feelings for me. G became worried about me and wanted to talk to me but couldn't. So she wrote a note and gave it to that guy to pass it on to me urgently. Now that guy was blackmailing me with it saying, "You never told me about her, but now I have evidence. Tell me the whole story, what happened and what you are going to do, otherwise I will tell everybody."

I knew he was joking, but anyway agreed to tell him everything and took G's letter from him.

I opened it and it said:

What are you doing there? You are there to study, so do your job. Are you having another affair now? That is probably why you drank Dettol. Sudhar Jao.

It was so innocent. I did not realize that she thought I was in love with someone else and so she was feeling jealous. Also, if she was indeed jealous, she probably still had feelings for me. I wrote a reply saying,

Whatever he told you is not true. Don't believe him. I will never do something like that. How did you even think I could do that? So, please don't worry about me.

She put forward a proposal to meet me and asked Amar to help me. I was in two minds and didn't know what to do. Should I listen to my heart or my mind? Should I meet her or not? Finally, the heart won.

Patna was eighty kilometres away from her house. Where would we meet? However, I could not deny her request.

I was thinking of what a date should be like. Could I even call it a date, I wondered. I was young and inexperienced in such matters. I wanted to gift her something as well. But I did not know what to give her. Then, I remembered the photographs of her and her family that she had given me three years back. Some were a little torn, but I decided to patch them up with scotch tape and gift all the photos to her so she could safeguard her memories. I prepared myself mentally to meet her and set off for home.

There were a lot of thoughts in my mind. Would she truly be able to meet me? Would it be the last time? Or could we meet regularly? I also wondered if this was the right time to propose marriage and see what she thought about it.

It was evening and the sun was about to set. It was winter but not too cold yet. I was waiting for her, sitting on a half-damaged wall at the site of a demolished property that belonged to her family, which was a little distance away from her home.

I was waiting for her alone and was a little scared. I saw her approaching with Amar. As she came closer, I remained silent and turned away from her, blushing. She was heaving from fear and nervousness and at the same time muttering, "We need to hurry, we may be meeting today but I don't know how long we can talk and it is so dark, I cannot see anything." It seemed she was questioning herself.

I smiled and said jokingly, "I will give you a pair of spectacles, then you can see."

"Very funny, *bahut bolne lag gye ho*," she replied, then placing her hand on my cheek, she said, "Just take care, I cannot stay here for long."

"Then why did you come here? It would have been better if you had not come at all," I said faltering.

"If you have anything to tell me, say it now," she responded.

"Nothing," I replied.

We were quiet for a while and then I said, "I have something for you." I gave her the photographs. I told her that I had fixed the torn picture and she told me that there was no need to do all that for her. She was in a hurry to leave, but I held her back by gently pulling her sweater. Then, she wanted to come closer to me but I asked her a question that startled her and made her even more nervous. Maybe she was expecting something from me but I had nothing but my love to surprise her with.

I told her, "Wait, I have to tell you something."

"What?" she asked in a low voice.

I was still not sure if this was the right time or place to ask the question because it was such a hurried meeting, but I did not know when I would get another chance. So I did.

Shaadi karogi mujhse? Jaldi nahi hai, sochkar batao, ye hamara future plan ho sakta hai kya?"

[Will you marry me? There's no hurry, just think, decide and then answer. Can it be our future plan?]

She asked astonished, "What kind of marriage?"

"What kind of marriage?! There is only one kind of marriage, a bond for life. I don't know of any other kind of marriage! Do you?" I tried to be humorous.

She was not in the mood for jokes and said, "I will give you my answer tomorrow in a letter."

I said, "okay" in a sad voice. How would she handle this situation now? What should I be ready for?

I also realized that girls are papa's *betis* first and boys will have to woo them as well. I was ready to take on that challenge.

I asked Amar to take her home. She was holding my finger and did not want to let go. I slowly slipped my finger out and sent her home with Amar.

I was not very confident about her, I was sure there would be a negative reply. When Amar gave me her reply the next evening I did not open it then and there. I waited until I had reached Patna and was in my room before opening her note. And, I was not wrong; it was a negative answer.

"How could you think about us getting married? It is impossible. My family will never let that happen. If they find out, they will kill me first. And, you will not be a happy man… And what about you? Your family is expecting a lot from you, your mother believes in you and is sacrificing a lot for you and you will commit such a blunder? They are dreaming of a grand wedding for you. I am merely a dream which will never come true for you, Nish… I have never thought about our wedding because I am bound by tradition. If you try to do something forcibly I will die. I cannot bear the burden of someone criticizing me or my family. So what if you don't get me? You are a wonderful man and will not have any problems finding a girl. My first and last wish is to see you become a good gentleman. I believe you can understand my pain and I can understand yours too."

I was prepared for the situation, but my heart did not understand. I sat on the floor, my back leaning against walll, feet stretched along the floor, no tears, but numb with despair. I realized I was fine till I began interacting with her again. I was back to being miserable. I let out my sorrow in a stream of tears.

Tu itna khamosh hai kyon, kya tere andar itna shor hua… ro bhi na saka, tu itna kya majboor hua …

Lafz bhi rooth gaye tujhse, ashq bhi sookh gaye tujhme.. basaya tha dariya apne andar, jane kaise ghooonth gaya.. aise chhua kisine, bina chhuye tu chur hua ….

Kuchh kah bhi na saka, aisa kya majboor hua…

[Why are you so silent? Is fury clamoring within you? You cannot even weep, what has made you so helpless? Words are offended with you; tears have dried up within you… You held an ocean in your heart, how did you drink it all up? Did someone touch you so profoundly? That you shattered without a touch and said not a single word…]

Chasing a
Fictitious Dream

She loves me... she loves me not. Her appearance in my life seemed like a sea tide; it was impossible for it to stay on the shore forever. She had not thought about asking me if we could find a solution and get married. Although I had expected this deep in my heart, it was still painful to actually experience it. It was one of the toughest times of my life. I was totally discouraged and had no idea how to remove her memories from my mind. There were many other challenges in front of me – exams, studies and creating a path for a good future. I had no help from anybody or even from my own heart or mind. But there was faith, and a belief that whatever God had destined for me would be good.

This was the second time that she had given up without a discussion. I was sure this time she would never return. From now on, we would be strangers. I swore that my focus would be on my future goals and objectives.

I had appeared for quite a few engineering entrance exams. When the results were announced, my best rank turned out to be from the exam where the invigilator had wished me luck. But still, it was not good enough to get me admission into any of the national level colleges.

I was at a loss, but then, I got a call from a college admissions counsellor from Madhya Pradesh. He was in the city, meeting students and encouraging them to get into their college. My friends suggested that I meet him and see if this institution was a good one.

I met the college representatives and they told me all about the college which was located in the Khargone District in Madhya Pradesh. The nearest city was Indore which was a hundred kilometres away. Everything they said about the college was positive: good infrastructure, one of the oldest colleges in MP, a reasonable fee structure, a good study environment and close to many historical sites, places of natural beauty and holy places. But, the college itself was located in a rural hilly little town and there were no job placement guarantees at the end of the course. However, looking at my scores, they mentioned that I would get my preferred ECE stream. And if I continued to have strong academic performance, they would help me find a job after graduation. Honestly, due to low self-confidence after their temptation, I agreed readily. I decided to pick this college during my admissions counselling.

On the date for counselling in Bhopal, seats for my choice of stream were filled in most top colleges. The other institutions where they were available were equivalent to the college in Khargone. My friends suggested that I choose one of the other colleges as they were located in large cities like Bhopal and Indore. Job placements were more likely in large cities. It was a little difficult for me to take a decision, because I had already given a commitment to the college counsellor from Khargone. My heart had guided me a little. I decided to stick to that college.

The next day, I was on my way to this college, which was three hundred kilometres from Bhopal. I was thinking about my past and also wondered if I had taken the right decision. I was wondering how

I would fare in a new place where I didn't know a soul. I worried if I would ever be able to overcome my past, and if I would be able to get a job after graduation. The college counsellor had assured me that they would help me find a job at the end of the four years when I would finish my course, but that was a long time away and who knows how well they would remember their promise!

Looking at the sky, I took a deep breath and thought God must have created a new path for me. It was a difficult decision to take, but taking some deep breaths and thinking of God gave me the confidence. The college appeared. It was located in a scenic place surrounded by hills, spread across a wide area, including the hostel and the playground. On the other hand, I was anxious about being so far away from home, all alone in an unknown place. Khargone was more than a thousand kilometres away from Patna. How would I survive here for four years? Who would be my friends? Who would understand me? I also had a tough past to contend with. So, all in all, it was a period of mixed feelings for me.

After completing my admission formalities, I was allowed to stay in the hostel for one night as it was too late in the day to leave the place. It was a hard, lonely night, spent in a constant state of dilemma about my decision. The next day, I left for home as college was not in session yet.

Soon it was time to leave home. I was happy and a little excited because I had got a chance to fulfill my dream. I was also a little wary as I feared this might be temporary happiness. It was different from my original goal, which had been to get into an IIT, but I thought I could do the equivalent of that after graduating with a degree from this college. I promised myself that I would work hard to reach my goals and never look back again. Nevertheless, I would question God, why despite the truth in my heart, I could not get the girl I loved so much. But, at that time I didn't get an answer from God.

I tried to focus on what I needed to do for my career. I had spent years trying to get into an IIT. Even though this college was not expensive, I still couldn't afford the fees and had to take a loan. Moreover, the college was not well recognized, so it was not easy to get a loan. There were many problems ahead of me and I had to focus on them rather than worry about my aching heart.

A new life in college began; it was a time to meet new people, new friends, room-mates, teachers and enjoy new experiences. Everyone was excited but apprehensive at the same time. We were introducing ourselves to each other and getting to know our college-mates and class-mates.

This was the first year and we were scared of our seniors because they would rag us. Ragging had already begun as we had entered the first session of the semester. I had a moustache and the seniors thought I was a super senior of the college in the final year. Later on, during one of the ragging sessions I was told to shave off my moustache. Some of them would ask me if I had completed my graduation and then come back for engineering and others would ask me how many kids I had. It was all in good fun.

There was a reason why I was in this college. My family had already sold some land to first finance my stay in Patna and then to finance my engineering course. So I could not just leave on a whim. The only option for me at that time was to complete my engineering in the best way possible and get a livelihood. There were many fearful thoughts in my mind. However, I was able to concentrate on my education and do well in my exams.

Ragging of juniors was an issue and it was something none of us could avoid. One day my seniors asked me and my roomies to copy some notes for the internal exams in their rooms. I was unable to go as I had a headache that day and told my classmates to please do whatever they asked. However, the very next day I was called by a bunch of seniors who started abusing me in college code words. I was about to tell them the truth when I was slapped twice by two different seniors; there was pin drop silence for a second.

I decided firmly that I wouldn't cry at that time but when I left that place after the ragging, I went to a quiet place to give way to my hidden emotions and started crying.

Then I saw someone had followed me, and asked me quietly once he caught up, "What happened? Don't mind this, it happens everywhere. We are seniors and we do this to train you and make you a strong and frank people. Why are you so worried and tensed?"

He had seen me being slapped but was not involved, so he came to find out what was going on. I explained to him why I couldn't go when the seniors called me the previous day. Then I told him to go away and leave me alone so I could cry in peace and let off my pent up emotions.

Then he said sympathetically, "Okay, take it easy, if you want to be alone, it is okay."

I didn't reply but when he started walking away, I went up to him and said that I would meet him the next evening in the same spot.

The next evening, when we met, he asked me a lot of questions and then said, "You know what your problem is?

I said, "Yeah, I am slowly realizing my problem and trying to solve it. And I know that it's only I who can do it."

He nodded and started explaining, "Everyone has problems, but who is responsible for that? We blame others for our problems, but they're not the cause. It is our mindset or thought process to fight our problem which is the real deal."

I nodded in agreement. Changing the thought process could help fight our problems, I admitted.

He was being very friendly. I was surprised to see him taking so much interest in me and casually asked him why he was giving me all this advice. He explained that my behaviour the previous day had made him feel that I had some other problems because no one else in the college had reacted so badly to the ragging which was quite common. He said that I didn't have to talk to him about any personal issues, but that I needed to remain strong. I simply said that there were some issues that made me react strongly to such things and tried to let it go at that. Then, we had a serious discussion and he explained to me that he had also made mistakes in life and then, accidentally ended up in this college.

He asked me, "Why have you lost so much time? What have you been doing all this while, before coming to this college? This is a serious matter. Think, contemplate about yourself, decide and implement it in you life… but just get yourself back on track. You are a dedicated person. Do something good, it is your life. You are free to decide and do what you want."

There were very few seniors like him who took the trouble to explain and motivate; most of them were only interested in ragging and making fun of us. He had asked me a valid question about why I had wasted all these years. But I had already wasted enough time asking myself these questions and thinking about my past. I didn't want to talk to him in detail about it as I felt it was useless to go over the same questions and problems again with someone else.

This was a time for introspection. I felt helpless and it was time to analyze myself, get inside myself and find an answer to the questions – What am I? What have I done so far? What have I got out of it?

It was a time to make a commitment to myself to work on improving myself and my life. I had been demoralized for a while, but now, with help from others around me and my own mental strength, I tried to focus on finding a path to happiness in my life.

It took me a long time to introspect and find out what I could do and what I had done in my life. I realized then that a challenge always inspired me; if I had tears in my eyes, I would have fire in my heart too to give faithful energy. Tension co-existed along with intelligence in my mind. When I was in pain, I also knew to anticipate spring, when everything would be beautiful. After much thinking and introspecting, I found an answer of sorts. My heart and my love were always pure. I had lost a lot of time in life, but there was nothing I could do about it. However, in the process, I had learned a lot and wanted to make these experiences meaningful in some way. I wanted to find ways to make connections between love, God, happiness, sadness and this universe. I decided I would share my thoughts with the world. I would express what I had learned through my writings. I may not know much about being an artist at this point, but I would take it up as a challenge and work on it with all my passion and strength.

That little thought excited me, and momentarily, I felt energetic. I thought, is this called positive thinking? Well, I tried to think about writing, yet did not begin. I had never ever written anything… a poem, story, article – nothing. Finally I picked up a pen and wrote down whatever came to my heart. When I showed it to my close friends, they appreciated it, but I did not know any expert in the field, so I felt that the feedback I received was not quite complete. I realized that I had to learn a lot, but how?

♋

Everything was going well for me when suddenly, there was another twist in my story: G came back into my life again. I had not expected this and was extremely confused. I wanted to focus on achieving something in life, but now I began to feel fearful that I would become weak and helpless again. But, love cannot be ignored and despite my mind warning me to be careful, I could not ignore her.

One day, I got a missed call from Amar's number. I returned the call, there was silence. I repeated 'hello' thrice. Suddenly I heard her voice.

"*Naraaz ho?* I am sorry. Don't you want to talk to me? I know what I did was not right, but how could you think that I do not love you? Think whatever you want to, but please don't think that I am not in love with you."

I was mesmerized. This was the first time I was listening to her voice for so long. I remained silent. Then, suddenly she stopped talking and exclaimed, "Thank God... we can have proper conversations with each other now."

She was talking to herself. "Thanks to Amar as well for his phone!"

"We should thank mobile phone operators who have given us a chance to come together again. Welcome to modern communication," I said lightheartedly, ignoring her previous questions as a happy engineering student. "Thank you as well for remembering me and calling me," I added.

"Have you finished your lunch?" she asked me.

I said, "No, I was hungry for a few words from you and it is fulfilled today. I can share a few words of mine as well."

"Wait, I have something for you to eat. You'll be happy after you have tasted it. Open your mouth and I will feed you with my hand," she said in a loving voice.

"Okay, what is this?"

"You do not remember your favourite dish?" she asked me and I tried to remember what I had told her.

"Are you eating fish right now?" I asked her with a smile.

She replied laughing, "Yes, I have some fried fish curry with rice that my mom made. I know you like fish, so I wanted to feed you some, Nish."

"Ahhhaa... thank you!"

She said again, "Open your mouth, I will feed you. *Ye lo, aaaaa karo aaaaa.*"

"You've started our communication by feeding me fish and having fish is a good omen to start anything in our culture as you are well aware. So can we hope for something good in the future," I asked her.

"Actually I am a little weak and so please forgive me if I go against your decision sometimes. But I am trying to find a solution for us to be together in the future…," G replied.

We had been speaking for an hour. The sun had set and darkness had set in.

After a while, I decided to bring up the topic of marriage.

"Well, I don't know where we stand as we had stopped communicating a few years back after my marriage proposal. I wanted to know if we could discuss that again. No hurry though," I said quietly.

For some time she remained silent. "You still have those things in your mind! If we don't get married, is there no meaning to our love? Our feelings have no value? Tell me, we are talking after a long time, shouldn't we talk about our feelings, and our lives?" she asked in a slightly angry voice.

I said, "Oh… yeah! Calm down. Sorry…"

We remained silent for some time.

Then I said, partly joking, partly serious, "Do you have something called feelings in your heart? I did not feel them as we separated a number of times chiefly because you decided that we should."

She said, "You are always like that. You can't understand one's helplessness."

I assured her, "I do understand, but we can discuss matters openly instead of making it an issue. Anyway, just let it be at the moment. I am sorry… we should be happy now," I said. "I will not talk about marriage, but we can discuss it openly and see if there is any way to overcome the hurdles of family and society."

She was listening quietly.

"Please do not discuss marriage again. Just discuss something which makes us happy," she said quite irritated.

"Okay, we will not… we will only talk about things that will make us happy," I said in a sympathetic voice.

I felt worried when she asked me not to talk about marriage but I decided to put it aside and act cheerful for the rest of our conversation.

Now, we could talk to each other more often, but it was still painful as she was not ready to make a commitment. Every evening of the ten day Navratri festival, I sat on the hostel rooftop, my back against the wall, watching the hills in the distance. There was a Durga Temple on top of the hill and it was lit up every evening because of the festival. I looked towards the temple and prayed, asking the Goddess to guide us in the right direction.

My headaches however continued and I tried different doctors and medicines but did not get any permanent relief.

G was angry with me for having so many medicines.

"Why do you consume so many chemicals? You get these headaches because you think too much and do not share your troubles with others. Why do you think so much? If you reduce stress, your headaches too will go away!"

"I am in love and I am worried because I don't know if I will always have that someone's support whom I love, " I said.

After remaining silent for a while she responded, "I will suggest a medicine, will you follow my instructions? Don't you want a permanent solution?"

Then she suggested that I take up yoga and stop worrying about our relationship. Her take on it was that marriage was not the ultimate culmination of love and if we didn't get married to each other, it was not the end of the world. It is not always necessary for lovers to get married or things to go in their favour. That was not the meaning of true love. There are many reasons and compulsions for us not to get married, but true love will always remain in our hearts. She also said that if we insist that we should get married to the person we love, then that is not true love.

Then she started telling me that I should take up yoga to help me solve my problems. I couldn't resist telling her that if she would promise to be with me always, all my problems would be solved. She had no answer to that, but from then on, she started teaching me yoga over the phone in the mornings.

My friends would ask me about this girl who was taking so much care of me. I would dismiss them by casually saying that she was my girlfriend.

Everything was going on well, and I was in touch with her constantly and also kept working towards my goals. I always wanted to keep reminding her that I loved her a lot. She was also worried that I may not be able to tell my family about her as falling in love and getting married was not part of our cultural tradition. She was also aware that I didn't want to disappoint my parents by telling them that I was letting myself be distracted by love when I should be focussing on my studies.

Once she told me that she would give me a surprise on New Year's Eve. When the day came, and I was celebrating the beginning of 2006, I got a call from her, saying, "I will be with you under any condition, whatever you decide. Your decision is my decision."

My emotions came out in anger. I paused for a few seconds and replied rudely, "You want me to suffer again? Are you not making false promises? You will go back on your words later."

She began to swear and started sobbing.

I was taken aback. "I cannot see you in this condition… please do not cry, smile please."

"*Tum nahi samjhoge kabhi mujhe,*" she said as she sobbed.

I said sympathetically, "Yes, I do and I promise I will respect your decision as well and will be with you, do not worry. However, it is not easy, so please think twice. But how come you suddenly changed your mind? Do tell me that. And it was nice to hear you sobbing," I added teasing her.

She laughed.

I wondered why she had suddenly changed her mind. Was it to make me happy for a while so that I could complete my studies without worrying about our situation? I did not know what was happening, but I was sure that her feelings for me were genuine.

I said to myself with a smile, "Fall down again but be strong and wise enough to control the rise."

I was in the second year in college now. It was the time to open myself up and get involved in the activities around me – celebrating, enjoying, talking freely to people around me. I wasn't a junior any longer. In the first year, I had been rather quiet and not many people knew much about me. In the second year, during the birthday celebration of a senior, there was a dance party. Years ago, I had seen G dance to the song *Tu cheez badi hai mast mast* from the movie *Mohra*. I remembered the steps clearly and so danced to this song during the party. It became a huge hit with my college-mates and I was nicknamed 'Chhupa Rustam'. After that, I was made to dance at every party and had great fun with my college-mates.

Around that time, an incident happened that made me question myself all over again. Ragging was banned in college that year onwards, but some of the seniors decided to ask the juniors to come to our hostel room and do some work for us. I was not part of this but because my room was used, I got caught as well. And, one of the guilty seniors even said that I had also participated. I never asked that guy why he had falsely given my name, but looking at him, I knew that he didn't feel guilty about it at all. Even though I was innocent, I had to face the vice-principal who warned me that I would be rusticated from college.

I was angry. I stood in front of the mirror and asked myself why did this happen to me? Why am I not able to control a situation for myself? I had to be strong and face whatever would come my way.

All this while, I continued to talk to G. Sometimes we would fight, at other times we would have nice long conversations and sometimes she would ask me to sing songs for her over the phone. But, in the midst of all this, I would always pray to God as well to help me remain unaffected if I were to come across any problems.

Sometimes I would feel that my life was dedicated to love and I would tell G, "Please do not desert me. If you do, it would be too difficult to take control of myself again."

She said, "I just want to see you become a gentleman and I am sure you are and will be."

I said in jest, "Never do anything which will make me a bad man. It is up to you."

She assured, "It will never happen. You are gentle and you will always be a happy man. Always try to laugh, no matter what the circumstances. You will find me with you always. I am with you," she explained.

She wanted to make me happy. I had to be successful and it would be very difficult to succeed if I remained a worried man. Her words were a huge motivation.

When I questioned, "Would you be able to wait for three more years for me? What if your parents find someone for you in the meantime?"

She replied making fun, "You are thinking too much and that is the reason you are losing your hair. Oh yeah I remember, there is one *asana* to grow your hair. Just rub your fingernails for a few months and have some amla."

I said, "Come on, I am serious."

She would come with some excuses if it was serious, this time singing a song from the movie *Veer Zaara*,

> *"Lahrati hui rahein, khole hue hain bahein... ye hum aa gye hain kahaann... palko pe gahre halke hain reshmi dundhlke... ye hum aa gye hain kahaan..."*

[The winding road beckons us with open arms...where have we come... eyes are shaded with dreams, where have we come ...]

I listened for a few moments, and said astonished, "Wow, Shah Rukh's girl, you sung very nicely."

"When we meet the next time, I will teach you to sing this song."

I sighed. "Let us hope we meet soon."

I repeated my previous question.

She replied in grumbling voice, "Be realistic, what can I do if luck is not in our favour?"

Then she surprised me by saying, "You know, I am going to Indore to complete my Master's degree, and hopefully join an MBA course."

I asked her laughing, "*Tum kabse padhne lag gayi*? After your higher education, how much will you trouble me?"

"I have completed my graduation," she replied.

"I know you passed your twelfth as I was with you till that time, but I don't know what you did after that."

Recalling her comment about studying further, I asked her, "Is that true?"

She said, "Yes, almost confirmed, but my dad has to decide where I will go."

I exclaimed happily, "It'll be great. We'll be able to meet, go on dates, spend time with each other in a big city. We couldn't do anything back home where it was so conservative. We could barely talk."

She also said a little more happily, "Yes, life will be better in a big city. We'll be working towards our goals at the same time – your engineering and my MBA."

"Let God make this possible. We will cope with any situation and we will have a fresh modern love story in the coming days."

"Please focus on your studies. I am with you and will inform you if there is some change in plan," she advised me.

I said, "I am doing well. The results have been good. There are three years left to make my results better. But if I lose you during these days, then I will regret it all my life," I shared my opinion.

She said, "Good, you concentrate on your present and do not panic about the future. I am sure everything will be fine."

♋

One day Amar called me to say that I had forgotten him. Mobile phones had brought me and G closer so we didn't care about him anymore, he said. He further said you are far away so I cannot even come to see you. After a pause, he said, "It seems there are many relatives at G's house these days. There is something going on." There was talk of marriage, but he wasn't sure.

I asked astonished, "Are you joking? Are you trying to hurt me?"

He replied, "I know you are sensitive in this matter, so I didn't want to tell you. Take it easy. Nothing is confirmed. Might just be rumours."

He added, "My girlfriend is married to someone else. I had deep feelings for her as well, but you never saw me depressed or worried. Take life as it comes."

"I can understand. I am sorry as I seem to be on the same path." I regrettably replied, in a sad voice.

What was going on with G? I was not sure how much of it was true.

The next time I spoke to her, I couldn't help asking, "Are you really going to study further?"

She answered, "I was supposed to, but now I think my family has changed the plan. I am also not interested in the course."

Then I asked her in a heartsick voice, "Are there other plans regarding you? Please tell me. I will respect your as well as your family's decisions."

"Why you asking me this?" she asked surprised.

"Are you hiding something? I'll be happy even if you tell me the truth about you and would respect the decisions," I said.

She said, "No, I am not hiding anything."

Then I asked, "Isn't there talk about your marriage at home? Haven't you and your family cancelled your future study plans because of this?"

She said laughing, "Yes, but plans have changed as I did not want that. I wanted to do some courses. I was about to tell you this, and my family has been talking about my marriage for the past three years, but still I am unmarried, right? Their decision depends on me. Only when I say yes that they will get me married. They want me to finish my education first."

"What is your opinion?" I questioned.

"I have no plans about marriage for the next four years, not until I complete my education. I still have to decide what kind of course to take up. My family is willing to delay my marriage plans if I enrol into a course," she said in relaxed voice. Then, she recalled what I had asked and counter questioned, "One minute… who told you about the discussions at home? Was it Amar?"

I said, "He is the only guy helping us right, so he updated me."

She said, "Oh I see, but Amar has changed quite a bit now, I do not know why. He is not how he was earlier; his nature has changed."

I asked, "What are you saying? I still trust him. Why do you say he has changed?"

"Please do not ask him anything about me. That would be better as I believe he is no longer interested in helping us. He has grown up," she said with a sad voice.

"He is still talking to me in the same manner and seems to be the same guy for me. Just that he was complaining that we seem to have forgotten him ever since we have started talking over phone," I told her.

She sighed and said, "Thank god! Please don't tell him anything about our communication."

I asked anxiously, "What happened? Just tell me."

She replied, "No, nothing much, just forget it. No need to tell him anything now."

I was wondering why she was suspecting a friend whom we had trusted all these years. I had my doubts and wanted to know the truth, but it was stupid to say anything to Amar at that point. After a bit of investigation, I found out that their fathers were rival candidates in the elections. I did not know what the matter was exactly, but there was something creating trouble between those two. However, I did not discuss this matter with either of them. I continued to remain neutral and talked to both of them as I used to before all this happened.

She was firm about this matter and told me, "Please do not say anything about me to Amar."

I had a deep fear in my mind that I would lose this girl. I strongly felt that she was hiding something from me as she would never tell me anything about what was going on in her family clearly. And I had no way of finding out. But, she would always tell me that my problem was that I was too doubtful. I would tell her that my problem was that I loved her too much and did not want to lose her. Apart from this, there was my family as well. My mother guessed that something was bothering me. But now, since G and I were talking regularly, it was evident on my face that there was definitely something on my mind.

When I went home during the semester breaks and vacations, my mother would notice that something was playing on my mind. She would insist that I tell her what was bothering me. I wouldn't tell her anything. She would then start praying to God, asking Him about what had happened to her son. Once, when I explained to her that I was fine except for the frequent headaches and that was the only thing I worried about, she asked me, "Are you worried because you get headaches frequently or do you get frequent headaches because you worry a lot about something?" I had no answer to that.

♋

It was the fifth semester break, a three-week holiday from college. I had planned to join a training course in Patna. I went home for a few days before the training. I met my relatives during that visit home. My mother secretly told my cousin to find out what was making me so unhappy. She was my younger sister and when she insisted that I tell her my problems, I could not refuse. I shared my troubles with her and asked her not to reveal this to anybody else. Then, she suggested I tell my mom something as she was very concerned. I agreed to talk to my mom and convince her that I was all right.

After a few days, there was a conversation between my cousin, aunt and her close friend regarding G's marriage as they were close friends of G's family. I was surprised and I asked my younger sister, "What is going on in G's home? Is there talk of her marriage?"

She said, "Yes, true, her parents have found someone for her and it seems she will be married very soon." Looking at my face, she tried to gauge my reaction.

She pressed, "She belongs to a traditional and very strict family. She will not go against her family's wishes, I believe."

I said quite nervously, "Okay, I know that as well and even I don't want to force her to do anything against her wish, but what does she want to show? Why did she not tell me clearly? This is the third time she is doing this. I never forced her to marry me… Leave it, I am fine. I've been true to her, so I feel some pain." Taking a gulp of water I tried to repress my sobs.

She responded in an emotional voice, "Brother, please control yourself, be strong because there are so many important things for you to do in life. We can understand your sorrow, but we cannot do anything as she is not interested in marrying you. Please take it easy as your mom is extremely worried about you; if you are happy, the world around you will seem happy."

After hearing this news, I became very agitated and it was hard to hide my true state of mind from the people around me.

When I reached home, my mother was even more alarmed. She began to force me in earnest to tell her what was going on.

This time, it was very difficult to hide my emotional state from my mother. I decided to tell my mother everything as it would be hard to pretend that everything was fine.

However, before I could say something this time, my mothers' sensors were already activated. In a very sad voice, she asked me, "*Sab thik to hai? Tujhe meri kasam,* tell me what is the problem?"

Before I could say something, she spoke again, "Is it regarding a girl? Who is she? Where does she live? *Kuchh to bolo.*"

I was silent for some time with my head down. Finally I said, "Yes, it is about a girl, but let it be, it is not a serious problem. I am happy because I just told you and wanted to let you know about what was happening."

I wanted to convince her but she became more worried and instead asked me, "Who is that girl?"

I told her everything about my relationship with G.

There was hush for a few moments. She burst out after a while, "Don't you have a sense of what is right and what is wrong?" And then suddenly said aggressively, "Don't you know how conservative this place is? Are you not aware of the culture and tradition which is more important than anything else?

I remained silent.

"You both wanted to get married to each other?" she asked in a hard voice.

I said in a low voice, "No, that girl is not interested. Ma, I am just in love with her and I am not going to do anything against you or her. She also has the same thinking as you have. I don't think she will marry me… but is there a possibility to get us married, Ma? If that girl agrees?" I asked her.

She said, "Oh… so your concern is that girl only? What about me, your father, our family and society? You do not even care! That girl is enough for you in your life?"

I had no answer for her.

She remained silent for some time and said, "Just forget her, you will find someone much better later."

I said, "But G will not be there in my life, right? That is what this is all about. It's not about finding someone better."

Now, both my mother and I had a number of disturbing thoughts crossing our minds because both of us had received shocks. I had just heard about G's impending marriage and my mother was aware of our relationship. I was trying to convince her saying, "Ma I will not take any wrong step which will make my parents feel ashamed. Please don't worry, Ma."

But still, she was not convinced. She said sadly, "Tell me where will you go after you marry that girl? What is your plan? Where will you live? At least tell me… I will not tell anyone."

These were innocent questions from a worried mother to her child. G and I hadn't even thought of marriage. But, my mother had this idea that once children grow up, they can do whatever they want. But, I knew I wouldn't do that without their permission. I would never do anything drastic that would hurt her feelings.

I said, "No Ma, I will not do anything against you. If we do get married, we will do it only with your permission and blessings."

"Don't forget her family. If you take any wrong steps, they may trouble us," she said in a worried voice.

I stammered, "Nothing will happen… I will not do anything, will do whatever you wish. Anyway, she is going to marry someone else now, so there is no point in talking about this. I am absolutely fine and will be so in future too."

"Is that girl fine about her marriage? Or is she unhappy about it? If she is not happy, she might take a wrong step. I am worried about you both."

I smiled and said, "She is more than happy because she never thought about marrying me. You may talk to her, then you will come to know her. She is more mature about this matter."

My mother and G used to meet regularly at the Shiva Temple where they both went to pray, but earlier they used to talk casually as my mother was not aware of our friendship or relationship. After I told her about it, G noticed that my mother's attitude towards her seemed different. Then, my mother informed her that it is me who her told about our story. G was stunned for a moment and then stated, "He told you about it? I don't know how many people know about this now. I am beginning to feel scared."

So my mother told her, "What is the point in being scared now? You should have thought about this earlier, before beginning your affair. Anyway, he is ready to marry you now."

G's expression revealed a lot after hearing the word 'marriage'. At that point my mother realized that G had no intention of marrying me.

She came home and asked me, how did you interact with her? Because, we don't have much contact with her family. Then she gathered that Amar must have helped me, so he became the bad guy too.

♋

My vacation came to an end. I had to collect my training certificate from Patna and return to college. My mother was more worried than ever. It was the morning of my departure and my mother was packing for me, but her mind was very busy fighting a number of thoughts.

She asked in a sad voice, with moist eyes, "How will you live? What will you do? I am so worried about you."

It was very hard for me to control my emotions, and not to cry too. I had to convince her I was fine.

I said embracing her, "I will never forgive myself if you continue to worry about me. Now, I will be more worried about you rather than my issue, because you will be worried thinking of me. You just stop worrying."

She asked, "How will you complete your studies? How will you concentrate? That is the reason behind your headaches. Leave aside the memories and stop thinking about that girl."

Poor moms; they always want their children to be happy and away from trouble. Finally she came with a bowl of curd and she fed me with a spoon. *"Bhagwan bala se dur rakhe."*

♋

While returning to college, I had to go via Patna after collecting my training certificate. I stayed in my cousin's house.

I wanted to hear the truth from G. I dialled her mobile number. "Is it true your marriage is fixed or going to be fixed? If so, why do you want to hide it from me?" I asked without a hello.

She surprisingly said, "Arey, it is not like that. Nothing is fixed. I'm not agreeing as I want to study further. My family will wait."

I said a little agressively, "Well, you have faith in your family. Your wedding is being fixed and you think you can get out of it. As for me, guess you'd have told me only after you would have got married or I guess you'd invite me to the reception and only then I'd get to know what's going on."

She replied in the same tone, "You change yourself, otherwise you will be like that all your life."

I slowly started sobbing.

"Calm down." A voice from other end said a little more emotionally this time.

"*Mann dukhi ho jaata hai*. Whatever is written in our fate will happen. There is no use in thinking about it and getting depressed."

I sighed, "You please don't worry, it is me who always gets hurt by reminding you about this matter."

She wanted me to relax and said, "Just calm down and stay cool, nothing will happen. You will be a happy man. Whatever will be will be. "

I said wiping my tears, "I will never cry again. I am strong enough to control myself." Then I disconnected the phone and switched if off. I wanted to be alone to pull myself together.

It was midnight and there was a temple in front of my home. Lord Shiva's statue was placed in the sanctum sanctorum. I glanced over and got emotional because I was begging for relief. I breathed deeply and tried to calm myself. After a while, I gathered myself and went in.

After forty minutes, when I switched it on, I immediately got a call from her. She must have been trying to call me all this while.

She shouted with questions, "Why did you switch off your phone? Oh god I was terrified! What happened? "

I calmly asked, "You thought I would take some wrong steps? Do not worry, I will not do anything crazy."

After this, she asked in a frightened voice, "Okay, I will listen to you and do what you say. But, do not do this again. I was so scared…"

I smiled and said, "I get emotional sometimes…."

She started forcing me, "Please tell me. I am sorry… at least tell me what your plan is? What were you thinking?

I said to her, "I will talk to you about whatever you want. I will not initiate any topic about me."

Now she was serious, "Tell me, what is your wish? Your plan?"

I joked, "The plan is that we will marry day after tomorrow. I am going to my place and you are coming with me, we will get married and live there together." She thought I was serious and she remained silent for some time. Before she could say anything about the plan, I said, "I got your answer. It's late now. We'll talk later, once I get back to college."

♋

My elder cousin who was a doctor was going to leave the city the next day. I went with him to see him off at the railway station. While I was with him, he asked me to share my problem with him as my mother had asked him earlier to find out why I was not saying anything to anyone about my relationship with G. I was surprised.

I said, "No, nothing… just a little headache teasing me, and I am worried about that."

He began explaining things to me, saying, "Mothers have a sixth sense solely to be able to find out her child's problems. You cannot hide anything from her. You are her child, she knows her child's pain. So you just tell me the truth. What is the problem?"

I knew my mother had not told him anything in detail, even though he was aware of my story.

"Do not worry. I will help you, tell me what is the problem? Is there a girl in your life?"

I was nervous.

He walked along with me to a tea stall to hear my story, but it was difficult to tell him everything. We had some tea and walked back to the train. Even though he was interested to know about my problems, there was no time to say anything as the train was about to leave. I wanted to tell him because I felt at least one person from my family, one who might be able to help me, should be aware of my situation. The train was on the platform and would leave in about ten minutes.

He said quite slowly, "Tell me what happened?"

The train started moving. I started moving along with the train, my cousin was standing at the door.

I said, "It's about a girl!"

"Don't worry. Just go to your room, take it easy. I will call you later and will help you," he shouted as the train picked up speed and left the station.

I wanted to hug someone and cry so that my heart could calm down, but that was not to be. I had to handle my situation by myself. Even the girl I loved could not understand my feelings properly, so how could I expect someone else to understand my emotions?

I recalled a couple of lines said by G and tried to move on, to make myself happy and get rid of the sorrows from my past:

Kya hua jo ek moti kahi rah chalte tootkar kho gya, Milte hain, hazaro milenge, ek se badhkar ek ...

[So what if a pearl shatters and disappears? Pearls can be found aplenty, each more beautiful than the other.]

In Search of Happiness

Almost half of my college life was over and I was about to enter into the third year. I got some moral support when my family members came to know about G, so life was a little easy. I had confided fully in my brother and he had been sympathetic. He had also assured me that he would help me in the event of any problems. Nobody could do more than that for me. It was up to me to make myself and my life better; to remain strong and focus on professional development. But by sharing my problems, I felt like a burden had been lifted.

It was a big decision when I had decided that I would write and do well in it. It was my ray of hope and would keep me engaged. G was still not married but the possibility of her marrying somebody else continued to trouble me. To change my heart and my nature was not in my hands, but I could take this up as a challenge and come out of it a better, stronger person.

I needed to throw out the negative and think about positive things, which could lead me towards a meaningful target. My family called me frequently to find out if I was okay and to motivate me to keep going. Although I was doing well, I still had sad thoughts and it was going to take some time for me to get over it completely.

My mother did not know how I was coping, but I tried to assure her, always saying she could live without a worry about me.

Sometimes she would be very emotional and say, "If you are fine then I am fine, you are everything to me. As long as you are alive, my world is perfect. It is all up to you, so please take care of yourself."

"All I worry about is you worrying about me, Ma," I told her. This was true love and without any ulterior motive. Endless love that can only be showered by a mother.

It was my mother or parents due to whom I was there. They had sacrificed a lot and I should not make them worry in return. Love does not mean that you make only yourself happy and make others around you suffer. I did not want to selfishly insist that I want to get married to G forcefully and let my mother and others suffer. Our relationship would eventually come to an end. I knew G would sacrifice herself for the sake of her family.

I needed a change within with the help of others, my surroundings, and belief in god. I decided to move out of the hostel and live in the city instead. I thought a change in my surroundings and lifestyle might help me snap out of my negative thinking and help me focus on improving myself and my career prospects.

Sometimes while travelling in the bus my friends would ask me, "Please share your story with us, we know you have a girlfriend." And, I would tell them, "I cannot talk about it here. To describe a story with emotion, there should be a beautiful natural environment around with flowers and trees. Otherwise, it is not possible for you guys to understand it." After that, they never asked me again.

My thinking was different so I kept myself away from these discussions.

Though one question always bothered me – why am I so different? How did I become like that? Maybe everything and everyone cannot be like me, but why am I not like everyone else in this world?

"Yeh dunia hamari tarah kyun nahi hai? Ya phir, main is dunia ki tarah kyun nahi hoon?"

This was the question in my mind when I realized I was different from others. Either better or worse, accepting oneself was an achievement.

೧೦

We started living a new life in my new home. There were four of us, but the fourth one Ashu stayed out most of the time because of his work. Sanju, Satish and I stayed together. Our landlord Goyal Uncle lived with his family. They had been apprehensive about renting the house to bachelors, but realized we were righteous guys and would never harm them. We also assured them that if they had any complaints about us, they only needed to inform us; we would vacate the house the very next day. Uncle encouraged us to just focus on our studies and fulfill our parents' dreams. If there was any kind of problem, he said he would help us in any way he could. Gradually, we became very close to them and we began to feel like we were a part of their family as well.

During our conversations, I came to know that he was a poet and a writer. I couldn't believe my ears. Who better than him to guide me? And he was a Hindi poet – close to what I was aspiring to be. A year ago I had started writing in Hindi and that was romantic songs, painful lines, feelings, whatever my heart wanted to express. I needed someone to gauge my work. He was the perfect person with his experience.

Goyal Uncle would regularly talk to us about our duty towards our parents and the importance of fulfilling their dreams. I was slowly coming out of my disappointment and focusing better on improving my life.

Uncle spent some of his free time talking to us. His views were something new and different for us and we enjoyed listening to him. However, I had still not told him about my interest in writing. One day I went to Uncle's room for some purpose. I entered and saw that he was busy writing something.

I said, "Sorry Uncle."

He said, looking above the rim of his spectacles, "No problem, you can sit here if you want."

I thought this was the right time to tell him about my desire. I said, "Uncle, there is something I have written. Whenever you are free, I would like to show it to you, if you don't mind."

He was happy to hear that. "Oh… you are writing, that is good to hear. But why did you wait so long to tell me this?"

I told him that I was just in the process of completing something. I was not a great writer so was a little nervous.

He said, "Come on… you write, right? And that is good enough. Bring your work to me."

"Can I bring it now?" I asked excited.

He replied, "*Haan, kyon nahi?*"

I ran back to my room, grabbed my diary and rushed back, panting.

He said, "Pull out a chair and sit. What have you written in this big diary? Have you filled all the pages?" he added looking at my diary.

I wanted to give him the diary and extended my hand.

He said, "You read it out to me yourself."

I started reading one of the poems in my diary which I had written a few months before, when I had started writing in my college hostel.

"Mat chalna un rahon pe, jin rahon pe tera ishq ka imtehan hoga,
Saya bhi tera sath chhod dega, Na mukkamal kabhi mukam hoga,
Itne kaante bhar jayege daman me, na nasib kabhi gulisataan
hoga,
Takdir bhi rooth jayegi is kadar, khuda bhi na meherbaan hoga,
Bas yaadein rah jayengi sath me, lafzon me jo na bayan hoga.
Doondhte rah jaoge khud ko, na nasib tera jahan hoga…"

[Do not move on a path, where your true love will be
sorely tested,
Even your shadow will leave you alone, you will barely
reach your destination
Your path littered with painful thorns, bereft of blissful
moments
Fortune will not favour you, even god will test your patience.
Only memories will remain, indescribable in words,
Searching for yourself all alone, even your destiny far away
from you…]

He listened with his eyes closed, fingers threaded behind his
head and legs stretched on his bed. After a while, when I stopped,
there was silence in the room.

"See, first thing, when you want to show your writing to
someone, you should always speak them out, especially poetry, as
that will make a strong impression on your audience. It will come
out from within you and people will feel your feelings, but if you
pass the papers to someone to read, they will understand, but the
personal touch won't be there."

He continued opening his eyes, "There should be power
in your written words, then it will be in your speech as well.
Whatever you have written is good because you wanted to make
clear your wishes. It is so simple and innocent, and express your

hidden feelings. But, there is something missing, which is essential for good literature. I will tell you what it is and guide you. You continue your writing."

I continued to read out my writing to him. He said, "These are good romantic lyrics and come out only if you have some special gift from god. Very few of us are gifted this way." And then, he suggested a few books and magazines for me to read and improve my writing skills.

I was happy to have found someone who had the same interest and inclinations as me – an artist whose nature was similar to mine. I was not aware of his personal life and he was not aware of mine, but I wondered if he had questions in his mind about why I was writing like this. I thought he may have guessed that I was in love and had suffered. He was a poet too and could probably recognize a heart when he saw one. More than anything, it felt good to share my thoughts and writings with another person.

I was changing my attitude towards my life. I could not change my heart, but I was in a mood to make myself happy in any way that I could.

I was determined to make a change in myself and so asked Ashu to lend me his bike as I wanted to learn how to ride it. Ashu spent most of his time outside the house, so we insisted to keep the bike with us. We assured him that we would take great care of his bike. He agreed and let me take his bike out for practice. My friends would joke that I was learning to ride a bike to impress girls. They were partially correct as I was learning this to impress somebody, but that somebody was myself. I wanted to do everything I could to feel better about myself and increase my confidence. So, I continued to work on my fitness and health, and began to try new things and learn new skills.

G and I were not talking much, but she would call once in a while.

She asked me sadly, "You've forgotten me, right?"

I sighed, said, "No, I am not trying to forget you, I am just trying to forget all the mistakes I made in the past, although love will be alive in my heart forever."

She further questioned, "Are you a happy man now? If so, that is good, just be happy, but do remember me," she concluded with a laugh.

I said, "Don't worry. I am better now and will try to keep myself happy. I've found many more reasons to be happy. This is an answer with confidence and I don't even have any complaints about you. Just be happy, that is my desire."

She wanted us to talk happily, as though there was no problem.

"We will be happy once you get married," I joked once.

She replied, "Why? What is there in marriage? Also, I believe you will not talk to me after my marriage."

I said, "Oh, what do you want? To get me into trouble again?"

She said, "No, a love affair is not the only possible relationship. There is also something called friendship."

I joked saying, "Oh, I've heard of friendship before love but here it's the opposite. Friendship after love."

At times during our calls, I would remain silent after one of our hopeless discussions about our future. Once she said, "Why are you silent? Do you think if you don't speak, the call won't cost you? Or have you decided to benefit the mobile service provider?" She would try to make me laugh.

I laughed and said, "Can we talk about our issue, your marriage?"

"You sound adorable when you laugh. Why do you want to become unhappy?" she responded, taking a deep breath.

I said, "Okay, I won't. You take care of yourself."

Goyal Uncle knew that something was bothering me and I had suffered a lot, but I wasn't talking about it directly and not writing about it openly either. Moreover, at this point, I just wanted to be happy in the life I had built for myself in Khargone. My roomies were unique in their own way. One was good at cooking, one at making girlfriends. I was much experienced in love and now totally focused on physical workout. We would talk about it at home and my friends told me that I didn't look like I had made much progress, even though I had worked out a lot in gym. I asked the trainer in my gym and he told me that I needed to follow a proper diet and be free from stress. Only then I would make progress. However, life was changing for me. I was talking to G, but our topics had changed. It was now all about sharing happiness. I was working on my goals and felt that life was on track for me.

One day, we planned to go shopping for gifts just a day before Diwali. Some electrical work was going on in Uncle's home, so he had asked us to get a few things as well. Sanju and I started for the market. I was riding the bike and Saju was riding pillion. We were in the market, and going towards the electric shop. What happened after that I cannot recall, but all I saw was complete darkness.

When I opened my eyes, two people, my seniors, were standing beside my bed.

I asked slowly, *"Main kahan hoon?"*

I found myself in the hospital but with no memory of how I had gotten there.

I repeated my question. They said I was in the hospital. They told me not to worry, not to think much and stress about it. Then I realized I was in a hospital but which hospital and how I got there was a mystery. I saw Sanju coming in with some fruits and asked him what had happened. He said nothing serious. He said I was fine, there was nothing to worry about, and he would tell me everything later.

I was being given IV glucose and I felt fine. Uncle and his family entered the door to see me in the hospital. They were very worried for me as Aunty had tears in her eyes.

I assured them I was fine. Uncle spoke to the doctor about my discharge and the doctor suggested that I stay there for a day. Uncle did not want to inform my family and worry them unnecessarily. After staying for a while, they left. After a while my friends too got ready to leave as a nurse came in to change my empty glucose bottle. They left saying I was lucky to have another family in the city. I said, yes, very few landlords are so caring and treat us as if we are a part of their family.

Later, once we were by ourselves, I asked Sanju what had happened. He said that a girl had suddenly crossed the road in front of me and while trying to avoid hitting her, we had fallen down from the bike. I became unconscious and Sanju could not revive me. People gathered around us and suggested that I be taken to the hospital. They moved the bike aside and parked it. There was considerable damage on the front of the motor cycle. Then, the police came in and took the bike to the station. Luckily, as Goyal Uncle's son was a policeman, he assured that he would help us get the bike back.

Everyone had left and I was trying to sleep after dinner. I saw there was a missed call from G. I ignored it but after the third one, I called her back. I couldn't talk much due to injury near my mouth. She started shouting angrily, "Where are you and why aren't you answering my calls? If you don't want to talk to me, I won't call you again, so tell me!"

She gradually calmed down and asked me quietly, "Where are you? What is happening?"

I started explaining the things one by one, told her about the accident, adding that I was fine.

She exclaimed, "What? Oh god how did it happen? *Tum theek ho na?*"

I tried to pacify and reassure her that I was fine as she said sobbing, "You are fine, right? I wish I could see you but it seems it is not possible in this life," she sighed.

I asked startled, "Why you saying so? What happened? You okay?"

She said, "Yeah!" and started sobbing harder.

I asked her to control herself and relax. "I am fine but if you do this, I will be stressed, which is not good for me."

She replied, "Rest as it is difficult for you to speak. I will call you later and will talk to you soon. I need to discuss something important," she sniffed before hanging up.

I leaned back on my pillow wondering what the future had in store for us.

∞

In the month of January, I was chatting online with my school friend, the one who had earlier told G that I had drunk Dettol. Suddenly he typed, *am calling you, we will talk.*

"How are you?" I heard just after receiving the call.

I said, "Everything is fine, you tell me what's going on with you."

We spoke for a couple of minutes and then he asked, "Do you have any special news from our town?"

I said, "What? No."

He kept repeating the same thing a number of times. "You do not know?"

I asked, "No, come on, please tell me now... what you are talking about?"

He said, "That girl, your girlfriend is going to get married. I don't have any idea about the date, but it is fixed for next month."

I was silent, completely silent, I was not even able to question him nor could I hear what he was saying any longer."

"Hello, helloo… Brother are you there? Please speak, what happened?"

I said, "*Haan,* yeah okay"

He asked, "What happened? You are not saying anything. Any problem?"

I said, "No, no problems okay? I am fine, I have some work, someone is calling me. Got to go."

He said, "Just talk to me a little bit first because you were completely silent after I told you the news."

I lied, "What we had was over long back, why should I worry then? You brought it up and then I was reminded of her. I am fine, there is nothing between us now."

He was worried now as he realized that even though there were no plans of marriage between G and me, I was still in love with her. He had helped me during our second break-up and he knew how strongly I felt about her. But, that was five years ago, so he probably thought I had forgotten about her. My silence disclosed the true state of my feelings and he then realized that the news had come as a shock to me.

I did not want to worry him, so I tried to pacify him. I said, "I was aware about her marriage, but was not sure about the date."

She had not informed me about her marriage – when she was going to marry, no dates, no sharing the news, no invitation. Anyway, I had convinced my friend that I was perfectly fine. But, I did not get any call or information from her; I was not even sure if she was really getting married or if it was just a rumour.

I assumed she was going to marry someone else. I felt a dark void inside me. I needed to be alone. I went to the roof. I wanted a deserted place to give way to my emotions and more importantly, to gather myself.

I sat in a corner with my chin on my knees. I began sobbing. Why had she not at least informed me? She could have at least called me and told me about it. It was very difficult for me to come out from the situation all by myself, but I still had deep faith in god. Whatever happens, happens for the good, I thought.

My eyes were full of tears, but I knew I had to be strong.

I told myself that the sky and the stars would hold me, comfort me, give me a place in life, a meaningful motto in life and make me rock the world. I looked up and asked god to give me strength.

Sar jhuka, ro ley ek pal, aansoo gire, mile mitti me tere gam..
Nazar utha tu dekh aasman, chand sitare raoshan hain..
Bahen faila bhar aagosh me, thamege wo bahen, hogi roshan teri rahen..
Uth chal de un rahon pe intazar hai unhe bhi tera, kar le tu teri aainke nam, chal de mita ke sare gam..

[Bow your head, feel your brittleness, and weep. Let your tears flow into the earth and bury your sorrows in the soil…
Raise your head, look at the sky glowing in the light of the moon and the stars
Open your arms, gather their luster into you, For they will brighten your path…
Move forward, they are waiting to meet you
Let tears soak your eyes,
And then, move on with a lighter heart.]

Trusting Myself and Finding God

There were a lot of frantic calls from my roomies. They wanted to know where I was. I did not want to tell them anything. It was dinner time, so I told them I would have it a little late, but they could have theirs. They need not wait for me. It was a time to make an even stronger commitment to myself because there was no point in wondering or finding out why she did not inform me about her marriage. Our relationship, first as childhood friends, then as sweethearts had lasted for fifteen years. It was not easy to forget all this in an hour or two. But I had to do it as soon as I could. I had no other option. I told myself this very sternly.

I believed in god's existence because during this toughest period in my life, I felt hugely supported by god. I had kept different pictures of gods with me since childhood. I took them with me wherever I went, especially pictures of Bhole Nath, Goddess Sarasvati and Maa Durga. I kept them in a small pedestal in a closet, each god looking a different way and when I prayed, I prayed to all of them. That time, I was not mature enough to know that god truly lies within a good human being, good work and in good thoughts. It was enough for me to realize that god is one but exists in our mind in different forms and names.

The evening when I heard the news that she had got married, I was in a lot of pain. I didn't know what to do next. When I got up the next morning and turned towards the pictures of the gods in my room to pray, I found Lord Shiva hiding behind Goddess Sarasvati.

I questioned myself, was this a mere coincidence that Goddess Sarasvati, the Goddess of Art and Knowledge was in front of Lord Shiva and directly in line with my vision? Was it an indication from Lord Shiva that the goddess was with me and I should go with the dream that I nurtured? It seemed like the message was loud and clear.

I was in a quandary. What was the use of my past experiences? I was writing about it in a diary but was it enough and would it satisfy me? At this point, I was only writing poems and lyrics, but I wanted to do something more meaningful. Would I be able to write a story about it? If I do write a book, who would read it? Nevertheless, I had a story to tell and I could spread a message through this story. This was Lord Shiva's answer to my desperate questions, that I could change my life by starting with small things.

I don't know who moved the pictures of the gods in my almirah and I didn't need to know. "Thank you god," I whispered.

♋

I had not interacted much with my college-mates, not even with my batch-mates, but I wanted to do all those things in the last few months left. Although we were not hostellers, and so, disconnected from the other students outside of class hours, we planned to go on a tour together. Most of them were interested in visiting a religious place. To my surprise and wonder, the place decided upon was

Shirdi Sai Baba's Temple. I had heard about Baba in different ways from different people. I had heard that no one comes back without Baba's blessing once someone has visited the place. It was inspiring to hear how Baba had spent his life serving poor people and that he had a lot of spiritual power.

There were nine of us in two cars. This trip was special for me and I was looking forward to the 'darshan' enthusiastically as my situation was not favourable at the moment and I needed Baba's blessings.

It was an eight-hour journey and we were on our way. We travelled all day. While travelling, we stopped at certain places for breaks. We could see that everyone enjoyed the journey in their own way, had great fun and indulged in different activities to cheer themselves up. But it was true that this visit was going to make some changes in me. Finally we reached Shirdi. Everyone had different views about Sai Baba. I was excited to visit Baba's Samadhi and pray for strength and self-empowerment. I was also thrilled to learn more about Baba's life and felt lucky to have gotten this opportunity to visit the place.

Every single thing was observed by me – what was written all around, temple, path, pictures and these inspired me to implement Baba's messages in my life.

Two words, *sharddha saburi,* meaning belief and patience encouraged me a lot. I did not go there for a religious purpose or to beg for favours; at that time I wanted to search for something which would change me and give me strength. I could not share these with anyone, but I had a good feeling about the place and Sai Baba. There was a long queue of people to see the Samadhi. When finally our turn came, it was not easy to hold back my tears. The only thing I prayed for was to be able to face my problems successfully. I had got a darshan of Sai Baba, so I believed there would be no more trouble. And, even if more problems came my way, I would be strong enough to face them.

Different people assume different things about god, religion, and racism, but I came to know god is only one and there is no meaning in classification of humanities. I know one god who drives the world and lives in good things.

In Shirdi, I saw two statements, *Sabka malik ek* and *Shraddha-Saburi* – there is only one god and keep faith and patience which I found relevant to my life. I picked up a book on the life of Sai Baba and some photos as souvenirs. We also visited Lord Shiva's temple nearby. I felt doubly blessed. After this visit, I felt very refreshed and ready to move on with my life.

♋

We lived in a residential area in Khargone and there was a girls' college nearby. So many college girls used to stay in the same area as us and in the houses surrounding us. Next door to us, three girls had rented a house together. They moved in there a few days after we had rented our house.

The girls were on the top floor of the building beside us and we were on the second floor of our building. The girls and my friends began trying to impress each other with my roomies showing each other in bad light to the girls in an attempt to gain their favour. Then, after a few days, my friends decided to choose a girl each for themselves, which required a round of interchanging for everyone to be finally happy with their selections. I was amused to see them having fun like this, that too without even talking to the girls yet. We were not sure what the girls wanted from us, as they were also showing some interest. My friends asked me if I wanted to make friends with one of those girls, but I said no. So my three roomies continued to watch the three girls living across from us and have fun.

There was another house beside ours where a woman lived with her two daughters. Their father had left them long back.

Their house was very close to our landlord's house. Both the daughters were smart and beautiful and they too tried to attract our attention. The elder one was blunt and spoke loudly so we called her Basanti. The younger one was little and pretty so we called her Chutki. She was studying in the twelfth standard. Both these girls were smarter and cuter than the other girls living on the top floor of the building next to ours, so there was some competition amongst my roommates to get their attention as well. I had big goals so had to ignore these small joys and didn't show much interest in them.

I noticed that the girls responded differently if I was there, especially the younger one, Chutki. There was just one house between mine and theirs with a lower roof level. One day, I was standing on our roof and happened to look across at her.

"*Kya hai?*" she asked me with a half smile on her face.

I had just looked in her direction once and she was trying to talk to me. I ignored her then, but she continued to say '*kya hai*' every time we happened to see each other. One day, I responded, "*Kya, kya hai?*"

I added, "What is your problem?"

She appeared a little scared and moved away, smiling.

The cook who used to cook for us, also cooked for those girls. When we found out about that, my friends started buttering her up so that she could introduce us to those girls. I was a mere spectator. The cook would tell me, "You are not like them; you are so calm and decent with no interest in these kind of stupid activities."

I said smiling, "Yes Aunty, I am not interested in playing around with girls. Just get those girls for them; they will get married to them, I guess!" I tried to make fun of my roommates.

Finally she disclosed their names. She told us one was Madhubala and the other was Tanya. She did not tell us the third girl's name as she stayed aloof and didn't show any signs of interest in the boys. However, we knew those were not their real names but we began to refer to these girls by those names. She also added that the girls were asking about me.

Who is that cool, calm, shy guy always wearing a cap, they wanted to know.

I said, "I know you are joking. Anyway, it's very difficult to impress me or get out some emotion about girls from me. Just help those guys as they are more interested in this matter."

There was a girl in my life but I could not understand her. Or better, a girl who made it difficult for me to understand myself. I was not sure if she had ever loved me as much as I loved her, and so I had a desire to know from the girls if they could really love someone as much as I loved G? And, that was only possible if a girl became close enough to me as a friend to confide in me that she loved a guy so much that she could not live without him. Or even if a girl tells me that she loves me as much as I loved G.

I felt that I had undervalued myself in G's love and no one could love me as much as I loved her and I would not get any positive response from any girl.

I don't have a problem with women or hate them or anything like that. People may think that I may hate women because I suffered a lot due to a woman. Although it was not easy at all for me to take command over myself after my relationship with G, I realized that all of it was not her fault. I was also responsible for what happened to me. Moreover, I had learnt a lesson so I had to consider that as well. I should not blame anyone for whatever happened to me. I should actually appreciate women as women had a big hand in changing my life and the best example of that was my mother. As human beings, we are supposed to love everyone, so that is all that matters to me.

It is good to rise up in one's own view and have some self-respect. Somewhere I had lost my self-respect in the journey and I had to get it back. There are many ways to search for happiness and if god blocks one door, there are many others that are open. In my case, I had academics. I had to study well and get a good job.

It was a difficult and challenging time for us. We had to do well in our academics in the last few semesters of college. We put in a lot of effort – having group discussions, and putting up posters with lesson content. But there was also time for fun at home. Slowly, the boys had given up hope of befriending Tanya and Madhubala.

They began to focus on Chutki and Basanti. Everyone paid attention to Chutki who would shout "*Kya hai?*" as usual at anyone who dared to look at her.

Satish declared, "I will make her my girlfriend."

I said smiling, "Okay, all the best."

Everyone would say she was doing this for me and I was going to propose to her. Ashu had a girlfriend, but still wanted to impress her.

Generally, I observed when I would be alone, Chutki would try to flirt in subtle ways. I felt uncomfortable, so I would just leave. But I did not disclose this to my friends. I remained slightly aloof and watched all their activities.

Once I was alone roaming around on the roof, and Chutki was trying to pull my attention toward her.

She said in a soft voice, "*Kya hai?*"

I said, stretching my arms above head, stammering, "Hmm, okay same question, right?"

She was surprised to hear me speak.

She was staying with her mother, elder sister, and a younger brother. Whenever she saw me, she smiled and acted naughty. She was always careful around her mother who was quite rude and strict. As she did not seem concerned about her studies, I once said, "Meri Maa, why do you still play with dolls at this age? Read your books instead."

She said, "I can play with anything, why are you so worried?" She looked sad and angry as her mother had thrown out some of her dolls a little while ago.

I said, "You are still talking about playing. I meant concentrate on your studies."

☋

In the evening, her mother invited us for a puja at their home the next morning. My roomies were ecstatic.

Next morning, when the doorbell rang and I answered the door, Uncle was standing there with the *prasad*. So the puja was over! That was our next question. Auntie had not given us a specific time. She had only told us to come in the morning and our mornings began at ten. I woke the boys up and told them that the puja was over. They were very disappointed. I gave them the prasad and told them that we were supposed to go there to worship god. If you think wrong thoughts, your wishes will not be fulfilled.

"Now, have Prasad with *shanti*, not with Basanti," I cracked a joke to tease them.

Chutki was eating something on her roof when I went up a little later, "Guava... you want some?" she asked me.

I did not pay any attention toward her, so she asked again, "You want to eat it?"

I said, "Oh it is your leftover, I don't need that. I already had some in the morning."

She said, "No, I will give you a fresh one." She took one fresh guava and threw it towards me. It did not reach up to me and got stuck in the middle roof of the other building, which was below our level with joints walls.

I said as I looked down at the fruit stuck between the walls, "It was not thrown by a true heart, you are a little weak, be strong."

I was watching Chutki's behaviour. I was not interested in getting involved, at the same time I did not want to be too harsh with her as she was much younger than me. Chutki was initiating some steps towards me. I did not want to respond but I did not want to restrict her either. I wanted to know what exactly her wishes were. So, I continued to go about as usual. I was winning her trust because of my straightforward behaviour. I had a lot of experience in this field, so nobody could say that I was not capable of having a girlfriend. If I had wanted it, I could have had a girlfriend in college too.

♋

The rainy season had already begun. It was the first rains of the monsoon season and we were all ready to drench ourselves in it. Then, we thought we would go for a ride on Ashu's bike in the rain and have more fun that way. On the way, I saw Chutki sitting by her window and enjoying the weather. When we came back, she was outside, running, holding a small boy's hand, spinning in the rain and getting drenched. My friends were happy to see her outside and started shouting, splashing water on each other boisterously. I was scared and tried to calm them down as Uncle was there as well on the lower floor. Who can stop them when there is a drenched girl dancing in the rain! To make it worse, they started singing a song,

"*Chai chappa chai…panio ke chhite udati hue ladki.*"

Luckily, they went in after much coaxing.

♋

The next morning, when I went out into my balcony. I saw Chutki sitting on the floor of her balcony, reading a book. I tried to get her attention by clearing my throat, then I saw that she was trying to hide behind the book because she was crying.

"I am sorry," I said. "What happened?"

She shook her head.

I said, "If you don't want to read the book, it's okay. Yesterday you were so happy in the rain."

She turned her head away from me with a slight smile.

I once again coaxed her to share her problem with me. But she refused and after some time, she appeared to have calmed down. When I looked at her, she said her usual words, "*Kya hai?*" and smiled.

I told her to just keep smiling. I did not know her problems, but I knew the sorrow of getting hurt and the importance of being happy.

Later she responded to me, "It is good for me to study. You are guiding me in the right direction but there are other problems in life. By the way, you are a gentleman and a good guy."

I said, "Thank you."

She seemed to be becoming emotionally attached to me. It looked to me like she wanted some kind of emotional outlet because something was lacking in her life due to her family problems. She was grown up, almost a year later now and looked mature. She had stopped her childish behaviour. She was serious about her studies, but still seemed to have some feelings for me. She refused so many proposals of love, and even my roomies had given up hope.

Unfortunately, I got caught, when she was trying to throw a chocolate for me standing on the ground. She asked me, "You want it?"

We were standing on the roof and only I was visible to her. I tried to stop her, but she threw it nonetheless and it landed in Satish's hands.

♋

When my friends came to know that Chutki was more kind to me, they began to feel jealous and began calling me Chhupa Rustum.

Meanwhile, Madhu and Tanya both continued with their subtle flirting. What made me so different in their view, I couldn't understand.

Very soon, I got a call from my college-mate Kunnu. Tanya had met him on the bus and she directly asked for my phone number.

"Shall I give your number to her?" he asked me. I said yes.

The news soon spread. Boys came to me and asked, *"Yeh kya gul khila rahe ho?* Give us some tips as well."

Many boys called me from the hostel to tease me.

"Honesty and being true to myself, that is biggest tip to attract anything toward me," I responded. I could never cheat anyone. I believed those girls were drawn towards me because they saw something different in me.

A few days later, I got a call from that girl Tanya for the first time. She explained, "I got your number from your friend. I believe you are aware about us. We wanted to introduce ourselves, and also we have heard a lot about you from cook aunty."

I said, "I know, you girls stay in the neighbouring building and aunty cooks for you girls as well. We've also heard about you people."

She asked curiously, "What does she say about us?"

I said, "Nothing bad or negative, just about being human beings. What does she say about us?"

She said, "All good things. She discusses you especially, you and your kindness and that you are different."

I said, "Hmm, that is the reason you girls want me to interact with you? Thank you for understanding that I am different."

She asked, "Can I ask you a question? I think it will not be too soon to ask?"

I nodded for her to go ahead.

She asked hesitating, "Do you really like Madhu? I will help you if it is really so."

"Well, no. I really don't."

I tried to convince her that it was fine to talk and be friends, but I was not serious about any of them.

Tanya talked to me frequently and it seemed like she was having more fun and interest in doing so. She discussed Madhu more, saying she must have some feelings for me. I did not understand why she wanted to talk on Madhu's behalf. Madhu could talk to me if she truly wanted to. I sort of felt good about myself though. I was not attracted to Madhu but I was happy to hear people have feelings for me. G's rejection of me had left me both disappointed and doubtful about my ability to attract love and good relationships. So, at that time, the fact that someone else liked me and respected me helped me a lot to build my self-worth.

It was good to hear people say that. I hadn't done anything for them, but still they felt I was different, kind-natured and spoke to me in a nice manner. I didn't know if they just liked me or were really in love with me. I couldn't have asked them either. But, it didn't matter. I was happy to simply feel appreciated.

As all this was going on, Madhu and Tanya decided to move to a different place. They did not want to, but were compelled to do so as their brothers were joining them in the city for further studies. While moving, they invited me and said that I was welcome to visit them in their new home. I thanked them and said they could ask me for any help anytime they needed it. After they left, the place seemed and felt deserted.

♋

A small lesion on my right toe caused after I had tripped some months ago slowly became larger and so painful that I was not even able to walk.

When I consulted a doctor, he suggested the only treatment for this was surgery. I was very anxious as I had never had even a minor surgery before, and did not know what exactly would happen. Moreover, the lesion was very painful and I couldn't put off getting it treated any longer.

Next morning, I reached the hospital and was told to lie down on the bed, after which I would be injected some anesthesia just to numb the wound. I believe there was an inexperienced medic, because after enquiring about the process, he stated that first he would inject directly into the injury. I was about to lie down on the stretcher, full of fear, when irresolute thoughts came into my mind. I took a deep breath to hold myself together. At that moment, I spotted a poster of Sai Baba on the wall. I was very tensed and scared of what was to come. I was in too much pain even before the injection, thinking what would happen? Would I be able to tolerate that much pain? Who would take care of me? Why did it happen to me so unnecessarily? The injection penetrated my wound like a missile. It was too painful to tolerate and I blacked out.

I woke up to find a doctor next to me, "Are you okay?"

With a dried throat, I said in an unsteady voice, "I am okay now."

One of my friends Arun was with me. "Thank god you are okay!" he said.

Meanwhile Sanju and Satish had also arrived.

I asked lying on the bed, "What happened to me exactly after I was injected?"

Sanju said patting my body, "Your body was so rigid, it wouldn't even move when we tried to shake you."

Then the doctor said he couldn't go on with the procedure as I had lost consciousness. The wound was bleeding and they were not able to control it at first. Somehow they managed to stop the bleeding and suggested that I get some rest for a few days.

Doctors suggested I leave, but as I began walking in the corridor, I could barely take a step. I felt so weak. So I sat holding the wall and my friends tried to support me.

I heard a voice and saw a lady. She said,

"Kuchh nahi Beta, ye kuchh nahi hai, bahut jaldi thik ho jaoge, logo ko dekho kitna peedit hain, himmat rakho."

[Nothing son, this is nothing, you will be healed very soon, this is a small injury. You are worrying too much about it. Look at others and see how they are suffering.]

One man was sitting beside her. His leg was badly injured due to some disease. They were sitting on the hard floor as they were waiting to get a bed in the hospital.

I said gratefully, "Thanks Aunty! I know this is nothing in comparison to your problem. I am absolutely fine."

I dared myself to face it and be strong. Using her words as fuel, I stood up and limped out.

Thinking to myself on how much this world was suffering, and how my problem is relatively quite small, I moved on.

My toe hurt badly. They did not perform the surgery that day and had decided to operate it later. During that time, one of my friends asked me to go to Shirdi with him. I had liked the place when I had gone there the last time, so I accompanied him. I visited the place in that painful condition. I was not able to walk properly, but after the *darshan,* I felt better. While returning, we stopped at Omkareshwar, another holy site. We planned a boat trip on the holy river Narmada. After we had gone a certain distance on the river, I put my legs over the sides of the boat and immersed them in the water to get some relief. I kept it immersed the entire time we were on the boat.

I felt perplexed to see that after a few hours, the color of the skin had changed. Over the next few days, the swelling reduced, the pain was gone, and within a few days, it fell off as dried skin. It was a miracle. Was it god who wanted to strengthen my belief in him? Whatever was the reason behind my surprising recovery, this incident only served to strengthen my belief in god.

♋

Madhu and Tanya along with their siblings invited me to their home a few days later. I refused the first time, but Madhu told me that Tanya wasn't well.

I thought I should pay her a visit as Tanya had just been discharged from the hospital after a check-up. I reached their house. When I entered the room, suddenly my legs collided with the corner of the bed.

Tanya ran towards me after getting up from her sofa. I was about to stumble but I said stopping her, "I am okay!"

She controlled herself and stopped before she could come and touch me.

"I am completely fine," I said as Tanya passed me a bottle of Dettol to clean my wound.

When I saw the Dettol bottle, I had a flashback.

I had some sadness on my face, but quickly I allowed my mind to recover. Meanwhile Tanya and Madhu came close to me and asked, "Are you fine?"

I said, "Yeah, I am absolutely fine," and glanced at Madhu.

I saw that she was standing away in the corner. She shouted as well but her reaction had been different when she saw Tanya approaching me.

I left the place after having some tea and snacks in their house. It was good to see them and I understood how they felt about me.

Tanya was better after a bout of viral fever. I was about to leave, when Tanya's brother requested I join them for a movie that evening.

After a big debate, I agreed to go. We had tickets for the movie *Golmal Returns.* It was a comic movie so at certain places we had fun and there was a lot of laughter. Sometimes Tanya laughed and kept her head on my shoulders. This was my first experience of a girl being frank and open. I was talking and sharing jokes with all of them. Madhu was confused about what was going on, and she felt a little uncomfortable seeing Tanya's behaviour.

I interacted with all of them. During the intermission we went out to have some food. Tanya tried to pay for us, but Madhu aggressively came forward and said she would.

I said, "You guys please wait, what are you all doing?

"Let me pay," Tanya said.

"You've already paid so much for the tickets, now let us pay."

Madhu took her purse and tried to pay.

I said, "Ma'am, it is not yet over, we have to go out again. Next time you can pay," I convinced her. I realized both girls had special feelings for me. I felt grateful and thanked them for the nice get-together!

☉

I was undergoing significant self-improvement. My headaches had lessened. I had decided to stop visiting doctors and having so many medicines. I decided to leave it up to god to heal me.

I was calmer than earlier and more focused on our future endeavours as our final exams approached. It was important to pass with good marks and find a suitable job. So, all romantic matters and girl issues took a backseat. We were all concentrating on our careers now because it was a crucial time in our lives. We had an option to get into the telecommunication sector with a reference.

That was our only hope to get placed, especially as recession was at its peak in 2009 though we also wanted to look around and try to get better options as per our core branch fields.

Ashu was more interested in the business of fixing admissions in colleges and jobs in companies through the back door after donating money. It was his talent and he felt he could earn a living from it. He was trying to get jobs for us as well without our knowledge.

Once he offered me, "There is a chance for you, we will offer you a job after certain interview formalities in a company located in Bhopal."

That was secret, he said, "I will try to get an offer for you, but please do not reveal anything to anyone for now."

His cousin was a consultant and he had connections in certain companies.

Ashu and I left for Bhopal.

After the interview formalities in Bhopal, he offered me few documents and said, "Do not tell anyone. This is not the final offer if someone asks you."

With a fake smile I asked "What is the benefit in that?"

He said, "Just go back to college and you will see the difference," he continued to explain. "We are trying for you to get in and you will get final calls, do not worry. After a few formalities, we will get in touch with you."

"No, it is not possible for me to lie to someone until it is not finally confirmed that I have got placed. I may be a hero for the others for some time, but I will lose respect later when the reality is revealed," I said to him.

He prodded, "Come on, you are overthinking. You don't have to say anything if they ask. Just tell them Ashu had referred me for this placement in the company."

I wondered what was going on. What was he doing? I decided to wait and watch.

When I was on my way back home, he informed a few guys and my roommates that I had got placed in a Bangalore-based software company. Now my roommates thought it is Ashu who referenced me and they believed it. When I reached, I saw everyone was looking at me expectantly, including Uncle's family. It seemed the most important question for everyone was: where are the sweets?

I wondered what was going on till I realized what must have happened. I had to pretend that I had got a job. It was an expensive act for me as I had to distribute sweets to everyone. I was much appreciated, especially by my friends and Goyal Uncle's family. I wondered what they would think when they'd hear about the truth. Should I disclose the facts? I decided not to and though that I'd deal with the consequences later. When I reached college after two days, news spread like fire and a lot of questions and wishes began to fall on my ears. It was difficult to keep up the act.

It was a very odd but wonderful experience. It was a different kind of experience and made me feel how sweet success was! People believed that I could do it because I was a serious, honest and hardworking guy, so it was not difficult for me. But, they did not know the reason behind my seriousness. I could and had to make this possible in reality. Now that I had experienced the feeling of success – albeit fake – I badly wanted to experience the real thing.

It was good for me to be happy, no matter whether the reason was real or unreal. I called Ashu and asked him what I was supposed to do with all the people asking me questions about my new job. He told me not to worry and reply as I had been doing. This was his business, helping people get jobs after paying a certain amount of money and he wanted me as one of his success stories. But, very few people were aware that my so-called job had come through because of his references. They thought my own work had helped place me in the company.

Next day, the HOD called me into his cabin as he had heard about my job placement. I thought that I would be caught now because he would ask to see the paperwork. I only had the offer letter given by Ashu which also did not make any sense.

I opened the door hesitantly, and entered his cabin nervously. He was seated with his colleague, the same person who had reprimanded me earlier in the ragging incident.

I was told to take a seat, as our HOD congratulated me. He was talking and at the same time arranging some files in his drawer. The other faculty member remarked, "Oh... he got placed? Good! I knew him. He was so serious and dedicated to his studies, good luck!"

I mumbled in my mind, you are wrong again! I am not so serious about my studies yet, but maybe I will be in the future. Almost everyone greeted me, but it was for my fictitious success. The faculty said some positive things but still I was the same person and had not changed much since my last encounter with him. It had been the sound of success which made me different in their views.

This was a curious situation. I acted very well in front of the HOD. Then, the HOD asked me to wait for a few minutes so we could go see the principal. Now I was truly terrified.

As the principal had to visit the city for some meetings, he was in a hurry. When I saw him approaching, I tried to handle the situation with minimal interaction. He appreciated me but the HOD was trying to add some more information saying that I was the first from our branch to get a job placement and so many things. I was scared but was acting well in front of them. When I heard they had to leave right away, I felt a little safe. Then, they told me that I should bring sweets and distribute it to all the departments. I had to spend a lot of money celebrating a job that I did not have.

The only fault from my side was that I had been quiet and let it be. I just watched the situation and enjoyed the moment as I felt it was more important to be happy and to learn from the situation.

And, it was also a commitment to my friend Ashu, that I would support him to make his business flourish. I was observing lives, not only mine but many more, and wanted to judge and learn the truth. Even I was not doing the right thing. It was a good experience to see how people like your success once you get successful. I was more determined to be successful in real life now.

After all this, I was sure that I would choose my career choice wisely after college. It made me stronger so I could endure the battlefield of life for as long as it takes to come out victorious. What kept me going was the thought that despite all the problems in my life, god had also given me options to overcome trouble and work towards a successful future.

As if this was not enough, my friends began to bug me for a treat.

There was one more reason to ask for a party, it was my birthday. Just celebrate! That was important for me. So I decided to give a separate treat to those girls and we friends would have a separate party. My friends decided to celebrate outside the college in the city. We would have a small birthday party in Uncle's home and then move it to a restaurant.

The party started at Uncle's home. Many friends joined us, we started dancing, and as usual on demand people asked me to dance to the song '*Tu Cheez badi hai mast mast*'. So, I started dancing in front of the people who had gathered there, including Uncle's family. A few children in Uncle's family were trying to make fun of my dance, but they celebrated and enjoyed the cake.

After this, I cut the cake amidst a lot of cheering. We left Uncle's place and headed to the restaurant. All the arrangements were in place. I didn't want to consume liquor as I had never tasted it and had no interest in it, but the others wanted to have some drinks.

They forced me to have some and also forced me to tell them about my past. Because they had started discussing the topic of love as it was my birthday and they were aware of my past and knew that I had a girl in my life who had changed me a lot. Everyone was interested to know more as they were aware of all this, especially Kunnu. They all became quiet and insisted I tell them my story or they wouldn't have dinner.

Sentiments pulled me back to the past, as this was the first chance to open up and say something without hesitation. I agreed to their proposal, after pulling from one of my friends a full beer of bottle and gulping it down. They said beer was not potent and I was in full control, but the rest of the guys seemed sloshed.

Rajeev asked me in an unsteady voice, "*Chadi kya?*"

I started reciting some shayari just to entertain my friends.

"Mujhe to pahle se hi chadhi hai koi, Is daru ki kya majal, ki chad jaye mujhper? Ishq ke nashe ke samne ye fika pad jata hai bhai."

[When I am already in a state of intoxication How can spirits have the effrontery to show its power? Compared to love's hypnotic rule, alcohol is mere froth, my brother!]

They started clamouring, "*Bhai aap to khiladi aadmi nikale. Hum to aapko gentleman samajhte the!*"

[Brother, you've turned out to be quite a player, we thought you're a gentleman!]

I said, "Yeah, love made me a player. By the way, a gentleman can also fall in love. There is nothing wrong in that."

Kunnu asked me to recite more poetry. He insisted, "We know you are a writer also, you write shayari and stories. Please say something more."

They all started shouting gleefully and encouraging me.

I said in a quivering voice, "Okay… okay"

I paused for a few moments, and said, this is for you *toote-phoote shabdon mein,*

> *"Ye dard ke kisse aasani se sunaye nahi jate hain*
> *Humne barood ko apne rago me aur dariyao ko apne dilo me pala hai*
> *Dil tham kar baithna e-dosto,*
> *Ijazat hogi unhe rago me phatne aur aankho se barasane ki,*
> *Fir tumhe bhi ehsas hoga ye kisse aasani se labon pe laaye nahi jate hain."*

[Anguish cannot be recounted effortlessly
Fire's fury is hot in my veins, the sea's ebullience is nurtured in my heart.
But, wait patiently my friends,
I will permit the fire to explode and flow freely out of my eyes, and you will know
This story cannot pass through my lips painlessly.]

As soon as I finished my words, friends surrounded and hugged me tightly in glee. I was grateful for their love and for making me feel light-hearted.

It was my first experience with alcohol. It had not left any deep impression on me, so I did not want to have it again. After the celebration, we started for our respective homes. I dropped a couple of friends at a time on the bike and the rest walked to a point from where they could get autos or buses. I dropped at least six people in rotation, but five were still there behind me. I had dropped those who were really drunk.

That's when I got a call from one of my friends saying that a few of them had been caught by the police. When I reached the spot, I saw one police vehicle in which three of our friends were sitting. There were a lot of people in the crowd and one person with few of our friends was surrounded by people. The person with my friend was the municipal leader of the city.

His political party was the ruling government in the state. I was quite scared. I was trying to ask someone what had happened and at the same time I heard that leader shouting, "Are you guys here to complete your studies or behave like this? You rascals, you drunkards, just call your parents, I will talk to them."

Kunnu and Sashidhar were caught. Two other guys had escaped in the dark and three were in the police car. I had to find out what had happened as the police had taken those guys into custody. After some investigation, I came to know this was the area where the leader lived. He had heard some loud noises and abusive words and had come out to check. The guys had been merely enjoying themselves, but their yells had attracted attention.

A few guys had escaped, but the police asked for the names of all the people involved. The guys refused to give the names when the police put forward the condition that if the guys did not surrender or if their names were not given, the ones caught would remain in custody.

I was scared but I went to the police station, and informed them that I was the chief person who had organized the party. Now the situation was in control as everyone was there, but now the main concern was to get ourselves released from police custody. Other friends who were not involved were trying to free us.

They asked for the reference of some faculty or management from college to free us. When one of our teachers heard about this and came to the police station at 1.00 a.m., they denied his request and asked for someone higher up.

We were more worried now, because the higher management of our college had to be involved and they would not be happy about such a situation. It might be a matter of politics because there were opposition leaders in politics – our college chairperson was an opponent of the political party member who had complained about us to the police. I tried to convince the police saying that it was my fault. I was the one who had organized the party. The police were enjoying the situation, jokingly trying to intimidate me, saying, "You stay in jail for a week, then we will let your friends go."

We finally asked friends to reach out to the vice-principal as he was our only option. We hoped he would help us as he was on good terms with me. So I told them I would try to call the vice-principal and see if he was willing to talk to the police and get us released from custody. We contacted the VP, apologized profusely for disturbing him so late in the night and asked him to help us. He was surprised to hear from us so late. Finally he agreed to assist us and came to the police station. He had a discussion with the policeman in charge and learned the reason. He came to know that I was the one who had thrown the party. One of the police personnel said that I should stay in jail for one more day, making fun of me as I was looking very anxious and worried. But I knew that the VP had handled the situation. We came to know that we were to be released soon with a warning. I had a chance to experience what it is like in a police station in my journey of self-discovery, but I surely didn't want that experience again, though it had been exciting.

The very next day, we had our annual college function and we had to prepare for it. There was an atmosphere of celebration in the college in the days after this incident, so we all forgot our past. Our farewell party was also coming up, (which was unfortunately cancelled later) so we had no time to dwell on our past. I was not able to participate in the college cultural programmes but I was helping in the preparations.

On the day of the function, we played a game. The rules of the game were announced on the speaker. If someone loves somebody and if there was a secret about someone that needs to be disclosed but hasn't been expressed individually to the concerned person, an announcement would be made. So students were announcing the names of the boys and girls who they were secretly in love with. I was getting ready for dinner with my friends and was moving towards the area where dinner was served when one of our friends Rajiv saw me. He was a volunteer. "You play this game, you love Nemo after all."

I said in a jittery voice, "No… no… I am not in love with her."

Rajeev said, "Yes, we know you do. Since the first year, you have had feelings for her but you were not able to tell her during the past four years, so I am going to announce it."

I requested, "No, please don't do such a thing. There is nothing like that. I just said that she looks like my girlfriend."

It was true that I was trying to tell my friends and seniors that her, Nemo's face, was similar to G's and that she was lovely and beautiful. But I did not love her and had never said anything about liking her to my friends.

I was trying to explain this to Rajeev, asking him not to make such an absurd announcement as she was present there. She was our senior but was still at college because she had to clear one semester. So, she was with us and it was the last semester for all of us. I tried to stop him. I respected her and feared that she would be angry and get hurt.

He finally agreed and said, "Sure we will not do that, don't worry, and enjoy your dinner."

I was standing in a queue with a few faculty members. Namrata who we lovingly called Nemo, was standing a little further away. She had already got her meal and being unaware of what was about to happen, was enjoying it with her friends. Suddenly there was an announcement, "Nish likes a girl since his first year in college, but he hasn't been able to reveal his feelings to her all these years.

Her name is… her name is…" There was a gap of six seconds, and people felt curious. I wanted to sink into the ground and disappear.

"Her name is Nemo."

As soon as I heard this, I choked on my food. They kept repeating it two or three times, and I began to feel tense, not so much for me as for her. I was worried about what she would think and how she would feel.

Nemo looked scared and shy as she did not have a boyfriend in college. She was asking her friends some question but they were all laughing, ignoring her queries. Later on, I found out that she was not worried. She was just trying to find out who Nish was. She knew me, had seen me around, but did not know my name.

Thankfully, there was no problem from her side and I took it as a game and some moments of lighthearted fun. There were so many reasons for sorrow in my life. It was important for me to come out of my past and make myself happy and playful. Incidents like these made up for the memorable days of college life.

♋

Once there was a poetry meet at Uncle's home, so he invited me to participate in it. I said I was not that experienced but he forced me and told me to just observe and see how it is done. I sat in a corner of the room, watching and listening. There were many famous poets and writers from the city and some famous personalities as well. I was listening to them carefully.

Then Aunty asked me to hand over cups of tea to them. As I was distributing the tea, Uncle said, "Nish, you join us."

I was a little nervous and refused.

Uncle said, "Don't worry, they will listen to you, your words, your writings and will give you suggestions. So go ahead and bring whatever you have with you."

I felt motivated and excited to present my writing to them. I waited and when my turn came, I read my pieces. I received some appreciation, as well as some suggestions on how to improve my writing. It was my first presentation as a writer and it gave me great pleasure to share my writings.

When the event was over, one of them called me aside and asked me, "Since how long have you been doing this?

I said, "I am new to this and am just writing whatever comes to my mind."

He said, "As a beginner, it is good, but you need to improve if you want to make a deeper impression. Do you have any plan to become a poet or writer?"

I said. "Definitely, I am thinking of that."

He said, "Just be in touch with us. We will help you."

Next morning, Uncle came to me and said smiling, "Someone's name is there in the newspaper."

I was surprised to see my name and the word poet next to it. It said that a student of engineering had started a writing career and expressed his views as a poet in a poetry meeting. So his journey as a writer had started and I was wished well by the senior poets. The guy who had asked me about my writing at the end of the meeting the previous day was a reporter, but he had not disclosed that to me. Instead, he quietly asked me for details about my education and writing plans and published it. I was happy and even Uncle's family was pleasantly surprised.

Ultimately, during the last few days of college, I got the prefix of 'poet' with my name. I was not famous but I felt it was true love which gave me the title of poet. Even if I didn't become one in future, even if I won't be in this profession now or in the future, it was at least a reflection of my past and I could not ignore it. I had to face it.

A wonderful experience of loss and gain was about to come to an end. We were going through the last days of college. Lovers were trying to sort out their future. Some broke up as for them it had just been a part of life in college. I observed Chutki, and it seemed she was trying to avoid me as it was almost time for us to leave. Guess it would be hard for her to handle her emotions as well.

Some on the other hand wanted to get married to each other. You could see couples in the libraries talking things out. Everyone was trying to find a job and secure their future and this became more important than romance and relationships. These were the last moments in college for us to enjoy as they would not come back again.

It was an emotional time as we were nearing the end of our student life. We would also be leaving our home away from home. We would miss Uncle and his wonderful family terribly. Cook aunty was also sad but blessed us and wished us a great future.

During those last few days in college, I spent a lot of time thinking about the years gone by. How much I had learned and gained, what I had lost and more importantly, how I had grown in this while. Now, I had reached another turning point in my life. I could see big changes in the near future and I was feeling very emotional about it. I did not yet know what the future held for me. I was a lot more confident now, but I was yet in the dark as I was yet to find a job. There were a lot of questions in my mind about my past and future but I had strong faith in god. I had lost a lot in the past, so there was no fear of loss in my mind. A fear of being alone and how will I suffer in the next journey did cross my mind though. I had to be confident and learn to move ahead through the difficulties in life.

I was feeling nostalgic about the things we had done together as friends in the past. Once, while on a tour, Sanju was eating peanuts in the car and throwing the shells out. He assumed that the window was open but it was closed and the peanut shells were falling back onto his lap. I waited for a while and then turned on the light and showed it to him and we all had a good laugh. Moments like these were flashing in my mind on the night that we were all packing. Four years ago, on the first day of college, we had all wondered how we would survive four years in this 'forest'. But the years had flown past, we had had a lot of fun, learned a lot and now it was time to part and go our own ways.

The next morning, we were all ready to leave. We had all planned to go together to the railway station and see each other off. We had arrived at Uncle's house as tenants, but had ended up as one big family. We were not only attached to our house owner's family, but even to the surroundings. It was even more special for me as here, I got the title 'poet' and this had given me some direction in life.

When we went to say goodbye to Uncle and Aunty, I tried very hard to stop my emotions, but eventually started sobbing. They were surprised seeing me in such a state and said teary-eyed themselves, "No son, no, don't cry. We will miss you and be in touch with you. We are always with you and will never forget you. You all are special and we will be in touch with you."

All that apart, I was no longer a weak person and had learnt a lot and become a fighter. I wiped my tears and managed to smile.

Finally it was time to say goodbye. We touched the feet of the elders around to seek their blessings and then we got into the cab. While the cab was moving, we saw Chutki, first peeping from her window and then come running out to the gate to say goodbye. I did not say anything but my friends waved and said, "Bye from Nish's side. He will be back soon."

When I looked out of the back window of the cab, I saw Chutki standing at her gate, waving her hand saying, "Best of luck."

Lekar chal diye yaado ki barat, sahma sa ye dil mera sahma sa ye sama..
Na Jane kis dagar, kis sahar, kaisa ho safar..
Thoda dare dare, todi himmat liye,
Palko ko nam kiye..bas chal diye..
Choota pichhe dilo ka mela, jaha hame khuda mila, hum khud mile,
Bohot yaad aayenge wo pal, jo diye hausla hume jab dil tha sahma sahma..

[I walked away on a trail of memories, fear in my heart, fearful of the world, towards the unknown.
A little scared, a little brave, I walked away with moistened eyes.
Leaving behind loving hearts, where I found god… and myself. Knowing I will remember forever
This place; those moments that gave fortitude to my frightened heart.]

Professional Life

An important part of my life was spent in college. But, now it was all over and it was time for me to look ahead. I had to create a future, free of problems, even though my past was making me somewhat helpless. I wanted to do something big apart from my engineering profession, but first, I had to find a job to support myself.

In college, along with studies, life was full of emotions and compulsions, but now, it was time to begin my professional life. And here, as I soon found out, there was no time or space for feelings, stories and the spirit of love. After graduation, I spent some time at home before working. I wanted to receive my parents' blessings before embarking on this new journey.

With the help of a senior, I had found a job in the telecom industry. It was the year 2009, the economic recession was at its peak and the telecom sector was one of the few industries still hiring people. After spending a few days at home and receiving my family's blessings, I left for my training and reached Coimbatore where my training was scheduled to happen. After being told we were hired and shelling out thirty thousand rupees for training, we were ready to join.

On the first day, our trainer gathered all of us and started explaining things about the job and the conditions under which we had to work. He explained, "It is field work and will never be easy for you guys, so before you commit, you should decide if you will be able to do this. It is not as if there are no other options in the job market, you just have to be able to crack it. In this field, there are two kinds of starting field work – surveys and testing. Survey is a bit difficult and is the initial stage and then after promotion, you will get a drive test. Or if your performance is good in the training, then directly you will get a drive test, also called RF engineering, but the main thing is both are field jobs and you have to work in the field for days and possibly nights also in the summer, winter and the rainy season, though all required facilities will be provided."

He was trying to give us a heads up because there were a number of cases where employees escaped due to difficulties. At that time, we all were excited and hopeful of getting the RF test.

As the training went on, it was hard to make time and find places to have fun. So, we just relaxed and refreshed ourselves with whatever was available nearby. Another important aspect of that time was that if someone received a call from the boss, then he was a lucky guy because it meant he had been completely accepted into the company. Then, the rest of us would worry about why we hadn't received 'the call' yet; was he unhappy with our work?

Yes, despite having paid for the training, we were still not guaranteed a position as we had to pass out of the training successfully. However, as I did not have much technical knowledge at that time, every moment was filled with new experiences and learning. It was also very important for me to learn how to implement what I knew. It was time for final results and project distribution. Luckily we all got what we wanted – drive testing to check the network issue and make them better and all of us were happy about it. Our training had actually ended abruptly after the theoretical part was over due to an urgent demand for new workers. So, it looked like we would have to jump straight into the job without any practical training whatsoever. Our trainer who had been our senior in college called us and was giving us final tips and encouragement, but he still had his doubts about me.

He said, making fun of me, "You are leaving and getting away from me, right? But I will not leave you so easily. Just stay here if you feel you need more training. I am not sure if you will be able to stay in this field for a long time." He had judged that I was not very confident.

I said confidently, "I will try my best. I have to do this."

He had been more interactive and friendly in college, but here he was a professional, so he tried to train us strictly and sometimes we were not happy about this. He tried to explain that we were all together now, but later we friends would be at different places and I may have to work alone. Then, suddenly he smiled and said, "I am kidding. For now, you have to go to Bangalore together. There your Project Manager will decide your job locations and send you where you need to go."

That was the last day of our training, and that evening we left Coimbatore for Bangalore.

I was still in touch with my previous landlord, Goyal Uncle and his family as well as Madhu and Tanya over the phone. In fact, Madhu and Tanya would call from time to time and tell me that they would not let me go so easily. I would tell them that if they had some dangerous plans in mind, they should inform me. It was all in fun that helped me remain happy so far away from home. I had moved out of my parents' house at a very young age and so hadn't had much time to spend with them. After that I always went back home for short visits. But still, my family's support and encouragement had always been there for me and this made me feel blessed.

My professional life had not quite started yet, but we were all set to move to Bangalore after the training. The nature of our work was very different. It was not the government sector, nor was it the IT industry. It was a different kind of fieldwork and the only parallel I can think of is the army. During our college days, we thought working would be enjoyable. During our training days, we slowly began to get a taste of reality. After training, once we were on the job, we fully realized the truth of what it meant to be a professional employee.

Finally we left Coimbatore, travelled overnight and reached Bangalore early in the morning. We had to immediately report to the manager, without even finding a place to refresh ourselves or have breakfast. He gave us an overview of what was expected of us and informed us that we would discuss it in detail after lunch, which sounded a little mysterious to us. Then, we started hunting for a place to have lunch. As we had been in the south for more than three months now, we had gotten used to the food a little bit but we all wanted to shift to the north as soon as we could do so. But, at this point, everything was a big question mark. Many engineers were already out there, working in the field. We were all struggling to cope with the change in environment, food, and dealing with adjustment issues.

We hadn't completed our training and that was the biggest issue here. Due to urgent manpower requirement, our trainers were asked to send us to Bangalore immediately. From here, we would all be sent to different places. We were anxious about this too as we felt that the day after our arrival in Bangalore, we would be sent to our work spots. We would all be separated and who knows when we would be together again. We were feeling a little emotional about this, although while living together we had a lot of complaints about each other. But, this was the time for new beginnings, new experiences, a time to learn and earn for the rest of our lives, for ourselves and our loved ones, so we were conscious about this as well. Our professional life was yet to start and already everyone was thinking about bank accounts, savings, marriage, home loans, etc. Some of us had taken loans for education and training. We hadn't even started paying it back and people were already talking about housing loans. No one was even looking at girls now. We still had one more day to go, to start our career and we were all so serious and mature already! The irony was that we were all dreaming about our growth, development and success, while the reality was that our work would merely help us survive while the company would grow, develop and become richer.

Anyway, our manager called us for a meeting to announce our job locations. Tension filled the air as our throats dried up. We were holding our breaths, just to hear that we had been placed in a location of our choice. Bangalore – as it was considered one of the best places to live and work in – was a favourite. The manager started announcing names and locations, writing on the board with a marker simultaneously: Sachin-Hubli, Sanju-Mysore, Satish-Hosur, and Nish-Bangalore.

The manager added, "You will leave for your destinations tomorrow evening. Now, go and relax. All the best!"

I called my mother for her blessings on the first day of my job. She was very happy and wished me well. All my family members and neighbours back home were very happy too and congratulated me. I,however, had very different feelings within me. I could not disclose to them that I was unhappy even before beginning to work because of what I had seen regarding the job pressure and work environment. But, according to them it was a happy moment and there was a long queue at the other end of the phone to wish me and ask for a treat.

Well, we were not IITians and the company was not an MNC, but we didn't care about all these things. We simply wanted to be treated fairly and honestly. We had been pulled out of training early due to project requirements and so had not had any practical training under senior workers. And with only theoretical training under our belt, it was not easy to work like seasoned employees, without slowing down or making mistakes. If we made mistakes, we were threatened with escalation, despite knowing that we were untrained and inexperienced in the field. And this fear of retribution and the pressure under which we had to work made us make more mistakes. It was very demoralizing, especially because even when we did a good job and completed the work in time, there was no appreciation or gratitude. The coordinator only said, "Okay, do more and do it quickly…"

My life was busy and stressful. I was constantly working under pressure. Sometimes I would wonder how long I could work like this. Our trainer had told us that we would have to work in the field for a minimum of two years before we could become eligible to be considered for a promotion to the post of a coordinator. Assuming I am immediately promoted after two years, would I even be capable of working like this for two long years in the first place?

As telecom workers, we were paid eighteen thousand rupees per month, which was hardly sufficient to cover boarding as we were on the move constantly. Most of us were unhappy with this entire gig and our aim was to find a better position and get out of this situation.

Once in Coimbatore, I was walking along, looking at all the shops lining the road. A man, dressed as Mickey Mouse was standing in front of a showroom, smiling and dancing and waving at the passersby. He was trying to make the passing children happy and entice customers into their store. He seemed cheerful but it was a hot day and I am sure he was boiling inside his suit. So, who knows how happy he really was? I felt like that man. The way I appeared outside was not how I felt inside. No one can observe or read what is going on inside our heads, only we will know what we are truly feeling and experiencing. But, we can pretend that everything's fine while interacting with the world. In my case, I had to stay strong and happy as nobody else could do anything for me at this point. Even though this was not my dream job, I had to do it for the sake of survival and at the same time, keep my writing dreams alive.

Everyone has to face problems in their professional life, especially in the beginning. We wanted to give our best and be a model employee but the nature of our job was such that there it was normal for something unpredictable or unexpected to come up and cause a hindrance to smooth functioning. It might be a traffic jam or lack of access to the places where we needed to go or it might even be birds and animals on telecom towers. For instance there were places where eagles would build their nests on mobile towers and then attack us if we tried to go up there to do some work. However, this did not prevent the managers from expecting us to produce results steadily every single day, irrespective of the problems we faced. They would be surprised if we went back to the office at the end of the day without any output and next day we would have to come up with double the work output. So, sometimes we would end up working all day and all night. Even if you were honest and worked hard, the emphasis was only on output and no excuses or reasons for failure were acceptable. Experienced people knew how to manipulate the output to make it seem satisfactory, but we couldn't, and wouldn't do it.

Sometimes, we needed to climb up the towers to do our work. Usually, we had helpers who would do the actual climbing, but in rare cases, if they were not able to do the work, we would climb up to finish the same. A lot of these towers, especially in remote areas, had eagles' nests on them and they would try their best to prevent human beings from going up into their territory. Even in such cases we were told to manage the situation with no external help. And, I would think, we barely manage to solve whatever problems we have with human beings, now they want us to handle birds and animals too!

Once, in a particularly bad situation, I was restraining my helper to climb but he wanted to try and tried two or three times, but the birds were so dutiful towards their family, they would come and directly try to peck him on the head. We had also been told that the climbers would be provided with safety belts, but we never saw these belts. Even if we were given safety belts, our heads would still have been exposed to bird attacks. The standard answer we received from the management, when we expressed our concerns about this was, "Try to manage it."

Many cases of eagle-infested towers were temporarily ignored, as the managers also knew that it was difficult to work on towers where eagles were nesting. But, they couldn't be ignored forever. Sometimes, we also involved the client to find a solution to some of our problems. For instance, we wanted a permanent solution for the eagle case because many times we were pressurized to work on critical sites despite the presence of nesting eagles and it was very dangerous. Once, one of our helpers was attacked on the head by an eagle while trying to go up the tower. There was a special team to remove these eagles' nests, but for whatever reason, they were not always deployed. Slowly we became habituated to working with the birds around. No matter how much we tried, in the case of eagle's nests, client involvement and nest removing was not always possible. So, we would try to work by scaring away the birds with loud noises. The birds would fly up and just circle around us, crying raucously while we worked, waiting to get back to their nests as soon as we finished.

But in between all this, we poor engineers were crushed. Slowly we became aware about the reality of working for these sub vendor companies. I worked patiently, despite many instances of escalation of problems. At the same time, I was trying to quit this job and find something better to do.

My mother had told me, when you get your first month's salary, just save some money in the name of god, and that she would have a puja at home. I was really in a turmoil at that time and no one was aware of how difficult the job was. Slowly I was getting weak and even physically unwell because of it. Initially I wanted to avoid telling them, but slowly they became aware that I was not happy with this job. Maa told me not to quit till I found a new job. She was a little scared and was worried about my health at the same time.

I was new to the city of Bangalore and did not have anywhere to stay as the company guesthouse was already full. For a few weeks I stayed in a hotel and caught an auto to work every day. Finally I found a hostel where I could share the room with others.

Due to the rapid pace with which we worked, without taking any breaks, my health began to deteriorate steadily. I was physically weak and was advised to take rest, but I had only completed three months in the company. And according to the rules, we had to have worked there for six months before we would be eligible for leave. Although we were supposed to have Sundays off, due to the heavy workload, Sundays were working days as well.

Initially I thought I was the only one frustrated with the job. But I found out that everyone was in the same state and wanted to quit because it was a thankless job with no future. I was feeling stressed because my past was different and I had a doubt that I was not relevant and fit enough for this work. My manager also told me many times that I was really not fit for this, but slowly I got to see that no one was. We all wanted to work hard but there should be rules and relaxation for employees as well as output for us like appreciation, improvements in position, and salary revision. But even senior colleagues had the same salaries as us. No matter if it was a small company or a vendor company, we knew the value of clients and we worked to satisfy them. There were rules and regulations for sub-vendors but there was a race between sub-vendors to be number one and make more profits, especially to get new clients and we workers were burdened heavily. Our juniors would call us and enquire about the nature of this job and if it would be a good option for them. We would say that it would all depend on how strong they were, physically and mentally, and how desperate they were to earn money. All of us who were already working here had the same problem. We wanted to quit but there was no time to look for other jobs. We had also invested in training, so if we left, it would be a loss for us.

Pritam, a guy who had done his engineering from a reputed government college but ended up in this company was in a similar condition as most of us working there. He had to stay on because he came from a poor background, had loans to repay and a sister to marry off. He was a mild-mannered, straightforward guy, who was always trying to avoid the manager. He looked scared and he always wanted to escape from the office because he did not want to see our manager as most of the time we poor guys were targeted by him. Even if there were no reasons to complain about us, he would pull us up. We were not mature enough to reply, so we simply wanted to avoid meeting him unless he called us for a genuine reason.

Sometimes, Pritam's behaviour in the office was kind of funny. He would be in a great hurry to hand over the report and to take his assignment from his boss for the day before the manager could see him and ask him questions. Pritam would run avoiding colleagues also so that no one could say or report anything about him to our manager. That was the fear of job security and managers, even if we were doing everything right; managers in this profession did not have the humanity to talk personally and appreciate us in any way. It was difficult to face the manager and answer his questions but if we escaped the office for the field, we were safe for the day.

One day, Pritam saw me in the office, with a half smile gestured hello by shaking his hand and as usual hurried away to finish his tasks and get into the cab to go to the field. Coincidentally, I too got into the same cab a few minutes later and saw him already sitting inside. He seemed to be a little more relaxed and said, "Hi, how are you? Long time!"

I said with a smile, "Just five minutes back you saw me in the office, you gestured something."

He said annoyingly, "I do not want to see that manager who asks unnecessary questions. I complete my job and leave. I do not want to interact with them; they only talk about more output."

"I know this is the effect of this work," I admitted.

He smiled and said striking his palm on his forehead, "I don't know for how long I need to work like this. I am totally frustrated with this job but I am doing it because I don't have a choice."

I said, "Very few people are happy. We are on the same page."

Life was very different from what it had been a few months ago while we were still in college. I missed those days a lot, especially the women in my life who had played a vital role in motivating me to fight for myself. They seemed to care about the good and bad in my life.

There was a huge impact of love in my life and that brought me very close to god and I felt the real existence of god in my life. Lord Shiva, Sai Baba and his words 'God is one'.

I was worried about my job, but more worried about why I was not doing what I had thought about, why I was not working towards fulfilling my artistic dreams. No matter how hard it got, I did not forget the passion in my heart for writing. Once, I discussed this with my senior and he told me, if you continue this job for a year or two, you will forget your dream. Uncle had once said the same thing, jokingly, "When you start working and pressure is high, you will forget this notebook and pen and this passion for art and writing."

But, I had learnt in my childhood that my love and god is with me during tough times, so, I can never forget this and wanted to make sure my artistic dreams came true.

Because it was a period of struggle, I was trying to get myself on track by jotting down my thoughts in a notebook even when I was on the move. Good words are written everywhere, but unfortunately, they are only read and not followed. If we were to apply it in our lives, they would be more effective. But, it is not done and so people don't change themselves or their circumstances. I always felt that I was responsible for shaping my life and found something to learn from every person, animal or thing.

I lived close to my office and used to report early every day. I hoped to receive some appreciation from my manager, but it never came. Some words of praise would have made me happier than getting holidays or a salary revision. At that time, most of us were hungry for sympathy and love rather than money.

Life was moving in the fast lane, so we did not have much time to talk to our colleagues and friends. Deepak, who had met us during the training in Coimbatore, had left the job after a few days of joining. He was not happy at all in the way they talked to us and put pressure on us. His aim was to complete his M.Tech from IITs and he had already started his preparations. We shared the same room.

Every night I would come in around 10.00 p.m. and would leave around 6.00 a.m. in the morning, so there was no chance of talking to him. I was always in a rush – coming home late at night, having a hurried dinner and soon going to bed as I had to start early the next day. When this became my normal routine, Deepak was unhappy and he asked once irritatingly, "What is this, yaar? You come so late in the night and you just hit the bed after saying good night. It's been the same for the last couple of weeks. We have not had a proper conversation."

I said with a fake smile, "I have to wake up early in the morning and your habit is to sleep late night and wake up in the afternoon. So sorry, my friend."

He advised me to quit this job too, like him.

I joked saying, "Oh okay, then who will pay your rent?" I was paying his share for the time being.

I added, "My condition is totally different and I cannot do that."

He advised, "But look at yourself... your health is deteriorating..."

I admitted, "I know, but who cares about all this? It is not important for them and I don't care about it either."

But I promised I would try to spend more time with him from that day onwards.

♋

My mother called one day to tell me that my cousin would be coming to Bangalore to meet a family for a marriage alliance. They were looking for a groom for my cousin. But this time my mother asked me to take care of him and accompany him for this. I was surprised and told my mother that my job had presently taken me out of Bangalore. She asked me to take leave as this was very important. I got a replacement and reached Bangalore again after almost one-and-a-half months. I was at the same place with Deepak, who was still preparing for his M. Tech entrance exam, so it was wonderful to catch up.

When I reported to the office next day, I was told that I had made a mistake because of which the network at certain places was missing. There was a problem with the device with which we calculate the proper strength of signal. I did not notice this problem, so the reports showed gaps in coverage. The manager called me and said, "I will write an email to the company that you are incompetent. You go home, your job is done now!"

I was very upset. I was wondering if this was really such a big mistake that I had to lose my job over it? I could correct it the next day, but he had never shouted at me like this before. Also, when seniors made bigger mistakes than this, he let them off. I was really demotivated and wondered whether this was truly my last day in office.

The next morning, I reached office in a hurry and was waiting for further response from the manager. I was waiting for him in the office, when I saw him I had a sudden urge to escape from the place, but thought to myself that one day I'd have to face this truth, so I stayed put. I was sitting there in front of him, but he ignored me. I was a little confident but still scared as I also had to ask him about my vacation. Uncle was about to arrive in the city in a few days. In fact, he was on the train to Bangalore already.

Next time when my manager came into the room, I wanted to ask for one or two days leave. I gathered my courage and asked him, "Sir, I need two days of leave".

"You want your job or leave?" he asked me.

I wanted to tell him my reason for asking for days off but he told me I wouldn't be able to get any time off from work. Now, I felt more confident that even though he had told me previously that I will be either fired or escalated to higher management, it would not happen because there was more work to do. So much so that he was not allowing me to take even two days off. So I said, "Okay sir, but as per the HR rule, I am eligible for a vacation after a few months, so that means after two months in my case."

He said, "Okay… good."

I was trying to weigh the value of what he had told me about my escalation. My confusion was about what was going to happen to me in that company. I was sure I was safe for at least that time, so I thought I would manage the family matter in some way or the other.

My uncle arrived in Bangalore. I was there to receive him at the station. I had some internal discussion with my coordinator and he agreed to manage for a few hours in my absence. I was free for half a day. He was aware I had not got any leave. I told him about the situation at the workplace. Deepak had accompanied me and my uncle learnt that he had quit because of the exploitative nature of the company.

"Why are you working in such a place then?" he asked, worried.

There was no end to this job; we were getting calls after every thirty minutes, even at night. He could see the kind of pressure there was. He certainly didn't look happy. I wished my cousins, his sons, " Best wishes Bhai. One thing is for sure, you won't be forced to be an engineer."

♋

After five stressful months, there was manpower demand in the Hyderabad location for a new project, which was managed by our college senior who was a project manager. We were transferred to Hyderabad along with a few of our friends.

We were all together – college friends who had all joined, trained and working in nearby locations. We celebrated like a cricket team does after taking a crucial wicket. Hugging and patting each other's back. So, we rented a place but bought just the essential stuff needed because we were never sure how long we would be in one place. We could be transferred anywhere at any time.

It was not all exhaustion and sadness. We had good moments too. We were a group of guys from all over India and Nepal. And we would all just sleep in a row on the floor every night, tired, each one making different sounds while sleeping. We'd joke and laugh and keep ourselves sane. But, it was not possible to be together like this for long. Rajesh, the boy from Nepal was the first to leave. One day, he was asked to catch the night train and reach Vijayawada in Andhra Pradesh for work early in the morning. It was winter and travelling at night was difficult. However, he had no choice and left at 11 p.m. Soon after he reached, he came down with a bad fever, asked for a replacement and went back to Bangalore. He did not recover properly and eventually had to quit his job and go back home to Nepal.

♋

The first official holiday we had at work was for Makar Sankranti. We weren't sure if it was truly official or if our manager had given us the day off because the client had said so. But whatever the reason, we planned to relax and enjoy the day. Vacation celebration started when we got the tickets for the movie *3 Idiots*. We enjoyed the movie immensely and it seemed to be directed at us! Thank you Raju Hiarani sir and team for making such a fabulous film at the right time for us. It certainly must have hammered quite a few thoughts into our minds.

The morning of the festival, I woke up to see many kites in the sky. Growing up, I had had a strong connection with kite flying. My friends were not very interested, but I went to see the kites on the roof. I wanted to fly one as well. I was surprised to see my manager at the shop. I was surprised when he wished me, "Good, enjoy! We will set our kites against each other."

We started flying our kites. Many kids were flying kites on our floor and other roofs as well. Initially my kites were brought down and the kids who cut them off were very happy. I said cheering them, "Wait kids, I have more kites," before I brought down some of theirs.

This made me nostalgic, as it had been my favourite sport in childhood and I had been beaten by my parents for this many times. I used to run long distances on the fields, trying to get my kite to fly as high as possible. Sometimes, it wouldn't go very high because the string wasn't long enough. But I simply enjoyed watching them up in the sky.

It was also necessary to check the direction of the wind because kites would fly in the same direction as the wind. And, if the wind blows towards my home, which was at the end of the village, I would try to bring down those kites. I used to raise the dust to get a clue about the direction of the wind, and also looked at the direction of the flags to check the direction of the wind and mark the kites coming towards my home for easy prey!

We would run fiercely to pick up fallen kites that had been brought down because it was not easy to get new kites. As a child, I had to struggle a lot to buy a new kite. Those moments were still fresh in my mind and flying kites that day brought out all the sentiments from the past. It reminded me of what had made me what I was today, what had played a major role in my life so far. I felt that I had to fulfil their value in some positive way. Suddenly I felt kind of discouraged, so I walked away from all the kite fliers and sat by myself on a boundary wall. The children started shouting, "What happened? Uncle, you are the loser now, is that why you are so silent?"

"I am tired, my friends will continue fighting with you guys. Let me rest," I replied, keeping their excitement alive.

Chali hai phir purwai, udh ja dhago ko liye sang
Hawa bhi hai sang, chal de lehra ke hoke mast malang...
Tere sang hai kai, tere rang hai kai...
Tujhe jana hai door, bhar le umang...
Hoja najaro se ojhal banke tarang, chal e-patang, chal e-patang..

[The wind is easterly yet again, fly away... Fly away with your cord behind you
Dancing in the breeze, leaping and soaring, fly away. Many more are flying with you, you have many shades to you...
You have a long way to go, keep close your passions and desires
Disappear like a wave, invisible to the eye... fly away, fly away.]

Finding a Path
to My Dreams

After the tiredness of the whole day in the dusk, I went in to do some writing. This was the first chance I had gotten in months to actually sit down and pick up a pen and paper. Now, my new friends found out about my writing and they suggested that this disorganized job was not for a writer.

After that, one happy, enjoyable day, life returned to reality. We had to go to the office to report and resume our work. At that time, we were also told that there were worker requirements in the north and so some of us would be sent there. We were all happy to hear that as we wanted to move closer to our homes. But, when the list of transfers came in, I was not listed in them. Everyone else left Hyderabad. Once again, I was alone and lonely.

I reminded my manager (college senior too) about sending me to the north as well. The language, food, culture was different in the south and I was struggling with it all. However, the manager asked me why I wanted to move out of here and advised me, "Ask your friends who have gone north what the situation is like."

I was shocked to hear about the situation in the north. They advised me to stay put. The work pressure was much worse compared to the south and was even more difficult.

The only pleasurable bit was that I got to visit different districts of Andhra Pradesh like Karim Nagar, Warangal and Khammam. I wanted to focus on my writing too, but that was impossible. I felt it would be wrong to look for another job because that too would take me away from what I actually wanted to do. I began to wonder if I could make it in Mumbai and get a transfer there. I could perhaps try my hand at writing lyrics or scripts too. I thought I should find someone who could refer me to the right people. An IITian who had inspired me to attempt for engineering from IITs in childhood, was working in Mumbai after graduating from IIT. I wrote an email asking if he could help me by referring me to someone relevant he might know in the city.

The reply I got from him was truly representative of people leading busy lives in a busy city:

Well, I am sorry, I am not alone with time on my hands. I do not even have time for my kids during their exams. You know your capability best and you should fight alone for your dream. I have no time to even read my business emails. With best wishes…

I did not take it negatively. He could not help me. I didn't know what the hell I was doing, but still I was so busy. I had no time for anything other than work. He was an IIT graduate, working at the managerial level with a leading name in the industry, so I could imagine how crazily busy he must be. I could not do anything about my passion at that moment, but I could make sure that while waiting for the right time, I did not let it die. Although people said a job and money would make me forget about my writing dreams eventually. In Goyal Uncle's home, a writer had advised me, "Be firm about your decision. Circumstances may want you to keep away from your dream. It takes effort to keep them alive. Keep the ignition on and wait for the right time to convert the dream into reality."

With these thoughts in mind, I continued to work in the scorching heat of summer, in the wet monsoons and the chilly winters. Everyone was fed up and wanted to quit but the question was who would dare to take the first step? Finally, one of our friends, Satish decided to make a move. He convinced his parents, inspired by the movie *3 Idiots,* that he was leaving the company because of his ill health, adding that he would take a break for one month and then would rejoin.

Slowly the others followed suit, including Sanju. One day I got a call from Sanju.

"Did you get the shocking news?"

"No, what happened?" I asked frightened. I repeated, "Tell me, what happened?"

He sighed and said, "Kalia is no more; he passed away today in the hospital."

It couldn't be true. "Please do not joke about such matters," I replied.

He said softly, "I am serious, why would I joke about such news?"

I felt numb. "*Kya?* Oh my god! How did this happen? Sanju said he was in the hospital, what happened exactly?"

Satish said, "He was also working for some vendor's company. That night he had to tend to a problem at four in the morning. He met with an accident when he was travelling to the site on his bike. He was in coma in the hospital for a few days but sadly did not make it."

He was very decent and mild natured and hurried to finish any assignment or job, even during our college days. He hated missing deadlines. He was keen and passionate and wanted to study further, but alas, that was not to be.

That was the end of an engineer's dream. He must have had dreams about his future, but it ended with him giving up his life.

He was also working for a private vendor and must have been under tremendous pressure. Was he working under pressure like us? Or did he have some other issues? Anyway, we lost him, whatever may be the reason. In college, he had been my only friend from my home town. He had helped me a lot by getting me medicines for my frequent headaches and anxiety and we used to travel home together. Will miss you my sweet fellow. RIP!

♋

A separate happy group had formed in Delhi, the members being those who had quit. They were now planning their future. The job was taking its toll on me. They asked me to quit, but I wanted to make sure that I had some other option well in hand before quitting.

I badly needed a break as I had been working non-stop for almost a year in all kinds of weather. I had frequent back pains, fever and headaches. I could not ignore them any longer and asked my manager for leave. "How long have you been working here?" he asked me.

I said, "Eleven months without a break."

He said according to HR rules, there is no leave till after one year.

"You go on leave next month. There is no replacement now."

I was working in Hyderabad at this time and after one month, when I was eligible for some vacation time, I happily planned to visit my native place.

I had saved some money for the puja my mother had asked me to. It felt good to pray to god. I was ill and weak and my parents were not happy at all. They wanted me to quit as well. I extended my vacation by a few more days as I really needed more rest.

This was the same place where I had spent my childhood, so there were a lot of emotional memories that gave me the strength to keep fighting.

I recalled those days, when I roamed around school and was wishing for those days to come back again. I remembered G and what I had undergone for love. I did not want to blame anyone and wanted to overcome it. But for me she still existed in the wind, streets, and school classrooms of the town I grew up in.

I had not yet recovered my health completely but I had to join work. My parents did not want me to go in such a state, but I had no choice.

I started the journey in a sour mood and reached Hyderabad with irresolute feet at 10 p.m. After reaching the guest house, a security guard in that building surprised me by saying that the guest house had shifted. And he had no idea where. I called my friend and he gave me the new address. I found the guest house but only to be told by the security guard that it was an office so I couldn't spend the night there. I was tired and feverish. And didn't have enough money for a hotel. So I finally asked the auto driver to drop me at the nearest railway station so that I could spend the night on the platform. So I spent an almost sleepless night in the railway station and in the morning when I reached the office, I was asked to meet the manager at the client's office. When I reached the client's office the manager said, "Oh! You came? We thought you will not come. Anyway, good to see you."

I said, "I was not well but I am feeling better now."

I got down to work as they left.

My old college friends who were in Delhi were planning their future. Some were interested in preparing for banking exams and some for IT. Those who were interested in the IT sector planned to move to Bangalore. I was not interested in the IT sector as I was not good in computer. I was more interested in something like teaching or a job in a bank.

Soon I was told to talk to my previous project manager with whom I had worked in the very first project. There was a requirement in Bangalore. Once again, I had to move to Bangalore, where I had worked for the first five months and restart a horrible life. But, it was a question of survival, so I had no choice.

After reaching Bangalore, my nomadic life resumed.

While travelling long routes and hundreds of kilometres in a single day to complete work and return home, I had time to dwell into the past. When I was on vacation, before I reached home, I had to collect some certificates from my college. I got in touch with my old friends there.

Madhu and Tanya invited me for a cup of tea. My friend Ashu accompanied me. Madhu made tea and it seemed that she was feeling shy. I asked both of them to sit together but Madhu wanted me to talk to her so that she could analyse if I still valued her. We had a short conversation and left as we had to go to Uncle's home as well.

I was warmly welcomed by Uncle and Aunty.

Aunty said, "We miss you and we have not given that flat on rent to anyone yet. It is vacant because we do not want to unnecessarily keep stupid guys."

I said, "Thanks Aunty! You understood us well and that is the reason we are here to see you again after almost a year now."

Then Uncle asked with a smile, "How is your writing going on? You remember or have you forgotten your paper, pen and diary?" He was aware I had a busy schedule at work.

I smiled and said, "Uncle, the same fire is still smouldering inside my heart. I have not forgotten my dream and that is the reason I am here to see you again. It is with your blessing I am still continuing with it whenever I have time."

He was happy but it was too short a time to discuss more details.

It was time to leave, but before that I went up to the roof, reminiscing about the past. Suddenly, I saw Chutki. She must have heard that I had come to uncle's house. Then, I noticed that she had vermilion on her forehead. She tried to say something but was not able to do it. I felt a little embarrassed and just raised my thumb and wished her the best. She had played a small but wonderful role in my life. She had made me realize that I was still worthy of being loved at a time when even I was ignoring myself.

Soon after, we left the house. This time it was different; we were not emotional. Time had changed, and so had our circumstances and we needed to keep our spirits up to move forward in our lives.

Those were good moments which I had after my vacation began and prior to reaching home.

It was good for me to see all of them and the visit was noted down in my memory. It also became a tonic in my life to inspire me to fight any circumstance, especially my present situation.

♋

In the telecom sector, there were serious problems in 2010. We had new projects and hence more work pressure. In 2010 when one of the big 2G scams in India was uncovered, all new projects were postponed or cancelled because most of them were illegally distributed spectrums/frequencies. So our business was down; there were no new operators in the market for competition. There were limited old projects, and our manager told us those who were working in a fixed location would have a fifteen percent deduction in their annual salary. The telecom market was going down due to the 2G crisis, so our company had fewer projects and was going in for losses. Other technologies were booming too but those were temporary markets. This news, along with the fact that we had to take a pay cut, demoralized us considerably. Now, it became even more important for us to find other avenues.

I had to decide on the right course of action for me but there was hardly any time. Work was still going on full speed and would sometimes continue till three or four in the morning, sometimes in forests, highways or mountains. So, although I had no clue in which direction to go, I had no time or energy left to explore options either.

When I was stationed in Hyderabad, I had reconnected with my old friend Ashok. Thanks to social media, we were able to find old friends. While I was working in Davangere, Karnataka, he called me. When I told him I was working in some remote place in Karnataka, he asked me how I was managing, because it is not easy to live alone and work in faraway places that are very different to what you are used to. He was now working as an upper level manager in a top IT firm and suggested that I move to Bangalore and look for jobs in the IT sector. I asked him how I could do that, because I was not a computer engineer. I was from E and C specialization and was clueless about software. He then guided me that there was something called software testing, which I could do without having any background or experience in the IT field. I was a little interested in this as my friends had prepared for this and taken up testing jobs. But then again, I was scared that I'd be stuck in another private company with no time for myself or my art. I finally made up my mind that I would spend a few more months in this company, earning and saving some money and then would take some time off to look for other jobs.

Now that I had come to a decision, I was less worried and more able to enjoy what I was doing at that time. On the days when we completed work a little early, we would go sightseeing. This way, I even got to see India's largest waterfalls, the Jog Falls… There were two other guys, co-workers with me who even encouraged me to have more fun by going to bars and picking up girls. But I put an end to those ideas. I did not want to create unnecessary problems by getting into drinking and girls and all that.

In the Shimoga district of Karnataka, there is a hilly area near Sagar town. In the rainy season, it is lush green with nature's beauty. I always made it a point to stop and admire the picturesque view. For a nature lover like me, it was a source of great inspiration. We also visited Kodachadri, another scenic place that comes alive in the monsoons. Small drops of water would caress me. I felt as if someone had touched me and these cold winds reminded me of my past in a strange way. My colleagues asked me to take pictures of these scenes but I told them, "Those pictures are permanently placed in my heart, so I don't need to capture them in a camera."

My spirit was at its peak and this natural beauty doubled my desire to escape from my job and do something more in line with my personality. Thank you god for creating such a wonderful world. When I see such places of great natural beauty, I feel that it inspires us to overcome our troubles. It feels almost as if god gives us answers to our questions through nature. I always feel good if I visit nature's fabrication. It opens my heart and helps me live freely.

> *Wo thi koi oas ki bunde ya phir aag ki chingari,*
> *Jala gayi dil me mere phir se koi aag,*
> *Mahsoos kar gaye hum kudarat ki is rachna ko…*
> *Ye parwat, ye hawayen, ye badal, ye jharnre, ye panchhi…*
> *Ye dhoon banaya jisne, phir se zinda kar gaya ek sangit…*
> *Utar rha mere dil me, phir se chhukar guzar raha koi…*

[Was it a drop of dew or a spark of fire? That kindled passion in my heart again. Nature's creation enthralled my entire being…
These mountains, these winds, clouds, birds and waterfalls.
This magical music is pure inspiration after so much pain,
My still heart is beating once again.]

Life, Love and Labour

Now the time had come to take a decision for my betterment. To quit the present job because I had some money saved would sail me through the next few months. So, without any formal notification, I returned my work kit and left, excusing myself on the account of ill health.

I started living with my friends, Sanju, Nitin and Deepak who had rented a house together in Bangalore. Ashok was very helpful and guided us on where and how to apply for jobs as we were all new to the IT field. He tried to place us whenever he heard of some job openings. Deepak had planned to move to some other field and was in the final stages of getting a job. Soon, he would move out of Bangalore.

I'll admit it was not great to be jobless, but we were all happy to have some time to rest and recoup after the harsh working conditions of the past few years. The others had been out of work for a while, so they were a little calm about it. But I had only recently quit my job, so I was still a little excited. For full one week, all I did was sleep and rest. The others told me that they had done the same thing. After that period of rest and relaxation, it was time to get a job in the IT sector.

After relaxing for a few days, I unpacked my only bag. All my worldly possessions were in that bag. I opened the bag sitting on the floor, and sighed as I took out my things one by one. There were two sets of very old clothes which I had used during my college life, a few toiletries, and most importantly, my diary. I did not leave behind these old clothes and the diary as they gave me comfort during all my travels. I had some good memories and now I could also spend some time going over whatever I had written in the past in my notebook at leisure.

I realized that I needed to go and buy myself a few clothes. We went to a mall and began to roam around the shops.

As I was shopping, I suddenly looked up with a start. I thought I had seen G. I looked up again in case my eyes had made a mistake, but it certainly was her. Quickly I hid myself from her sight. What a weird twist of fate! I was scared of appearing in front of her, in case she tried to speak to me. I broke down overwhelmed with emotions as our past played in my mind. My heart was pounding against my chest. Long back I had heard from my family that she had settled down in Bangalore after getting married. But still, I had not expected to suddenly see her like this. I tried to hide myself from her as she looked like a happily married woman with a baby sleeping on her shoulder. Later I realized that it was a baby girl. She was busy shopping and didn't look towards me. I escaped from the place. My friend Sanju observed my behaviour and asked me what had happened.

I told him that I would tell him later. I sped to the counter to pay the bill. But she was headed in the same direction. After a few minutes, I caught her looking at me. I wanted to become invisible. I ignored her and looked in the other direction. She was looking at me constantly, and my friends noticed that. I wanted to escape without talking to her. What kind of twist was this! That I was reminded of what I had fought so hard to forget. I recalled her words. "We will stay together; we will be in the same city, the same place but remain friends if we don't get married." Another time, she had told me that she wanted a baby girl. Now, it seemed that both her wishes had come true!

After seeing her, I couldn't get her out of my mind. I had to be patient and fight the situation, but it was harder because I was jobless as well. It was hard to forget all those things easily, but there was another goal – to get a new job. So I tried hard to forget the encounter. My journey in the telecom sector had taught me a lesson – how to stick to your work, and I knew if I could do what I did in my first job, then for my betterment, I could do even more.

Those days I was a little free, while searching for a job. I was also enjoying the surroundings, events, nature, people, and watching situations very closely. Small things made a big difference. I was trying to understand what was in those small things, and what they meant. I tried to learn from them and tried to implement some of these thoughts in my life. It was more important to learn lessons; it did not matter if they were from big books or small quotations.

We read so many books but they have no meaning if we don't implement some of those noble thoughts and ideas in our lives. I was in search of a job in IT so tried to attend some demos in a training class. There I met a few people with our friends; they all were discussing about study and training, but suddenly my eyes landed on a guy's t-shirt. I was paying more attention to the written stuff on the t-shirt, rather than the discussion about our classes and courses. It read

'Every successful man has a painful life.'

This thought was no surprise to me. It is not easy to make a life successful and almost everyone has a different kind of pain. The trick is to face it, get out of it. Written things are mostly true and all we need to do is truly implement them. It is not necessary that success will follow, but we can make our pain an inspiration of learning as an effort towards a meaningful goal that may lead towards happiness. And good work and success are very closely related.

In some ways, life was more difficult during this period as I had no income and my saved up money was depleting. Help from friends made me grateful and I learnt many things from them for survival. Ashok helped with money for a few months. I couldn't have made it without their help.

After certain attempts and rejections in interviews, I was disappointed. I wasn't being able to cross the first bridge towards my dream. There were many engineers like me struggling to find jobs, so it was never easy. Friends suggested that I take up a part time job while hunting for a full time job suited to my education and skills.

In most of the companies, I was almost selected but at the very last stage, I'd be rejected for very minor reasons. I kept wondering what was the issue here? Where am I lacking? What is wrong with me? I got to look at the sky and ask god, please forgive me for any mistakes I've made for which I am being punished now. I was about to cry, but I absorbed my tears within me. I had to be strong, so I tried to gather my courage and compose myself.

Those moments really made me upset. But after a while, I looked up while walking and said, "God thanks and excuse me if there is something wrong or there is something lacking in my preparation."

And then, I doubled my speed to the bus stop as it was a few kilometres from the company. Gradually, while walking, I was filled with a new energy and thought, so what if I missed this opportunity? No problem, I am sure I will get a better opportunity soon.

It was worrisome that I was attending all these interviews but I was not getting selected anywhere. But, at the same time, I was also getting better day by day at interviews and communicating my skills and abilities; that was a blessing.

♋

Sometimes, three or four weeks would go by without any interview calls and it would make us extremely anxious. I had got a call from a company for an interview. We were habituated to refer our friends for any interview calls, whether they decide to attend them or not. So, we all were there for this interview, including Sanju and a few more guys whom I referred for this job. After the interview, only Sanju and I qualified for the next round of interviews. We were told that we would get a call within a week for the next round of interviews, but we had faced this kind of situation many times, so we were casual about it. However, that same evening, I got a call asking for my details because there was a need to appear in the next round the very next day. Sanju did not get the call and he was upset about it. I had to prepare for the next round. The next morning, I got a call for reporting details but I felt desperate when I heard that it was to start at sharp 9:30 while I had been told the previous day that it was to start at 11.30. How would I reach on time? It was already nine.

Nevertheles, I hurried out with my shoes in my hand. I called them to say I would be late and they said they'd see what they could do.

I reached the venue to find that the process had already begun. The security guard wasn't letting anyone in. I called up the people and they told me to wait. I was frustrated because I did not want to miss a single opportunity. I joined the group outside. Some of them returned hopelessly. After a lot of pleading, I finally got permission along with a few guys to go in and appear for the interview.

Being selected is a different thing, but to appear after so many struggles was a different experience in itself. I appeared in the exam with almost more than five hundred candidates and was told to wait for the result in the evening. I would get a call if I got selected. I was quite comfortable and was waiting. I was neither nervous nor excited about the result. I was surprised to get a call from an unknown number. I picked it up and the words I heard filled me with joy. "You are selected for the next round; your next interview is scheduled for tomorrow morning at nine."

The next day, I went ahead of time. I saw that there were about fifty five candidates for the next round for the same position. We went through three more rounds of interviews, and collectively waited for the final results as the process was almost over.

It was time for our results and it was hard to be patient. Candidates' names were called and one by one, they went outside. I was sitting with my head down, mentally preparing myself to get ready to leave. Now it was my turn to stand outside with the others. When all the names were announced, a member of the recruitment team came and took all of us in a group towards the main exit gate. We were about to leave the campus, thinking he was bidding us farewell. As we were walking out, one of the guys finally asked, "Sir, you are going to say bye near the exit gate or will you push us out?

The answer we received was, "Oh no man! You are in the list of selected candidates. We are going to another campus for the next round of formalities."

"Is this the final shortlist?" someone popped.

He got an answer, "If you think you have not been selected finally then you will not be because there is just one formality left."

I could not believe it. I kept my hands on my forehead and my eyes were sparkling. It was evening time and the sky was shining as if it was in celebration. I looked up at the sky and thanked god. Sai Baba was always with me. I was almost sure that now I would get a job, but could not say anything until I had a joining letter in my hand.

I was delighted because I was about to get an offer from one of the top ten MNCs in the world and I felt proud of myself. It was still not finalized but since the HR had selected us, this made us confident that we would clear the formality on the part of the project manager. There was still some irresolution in my mind because we had faced so many situations like this. The next day I was there well prepared. I would get a final response from them after two days.

♋

I waited eagerly for the two days to get over. They did then, three, four and finally five days went by without a word from them. I called the third party for an update and was devastated to hear that the selection process was over. I was totally upset why this always happened to me towards the end. So many times, I had reached the stage and ended in naught. This particular case worried me the most as it looked like I had the best chance possible to get into a better company. But finally, all good chances are meaningless if you do not get in. My friends tried to console me in vain.

After a few days, I was in a saloon for my a haircut when I got a call from the company to collect my offer letter. I asked them to repeat themselves as I couldn't believe my ears. I had lost hope. I asked about the delay and he said there were requirements project wise and so he had to call me as my turn came. Salary did not matter that time, because my main goal was to get a job and work in a better environment.

Upon joining, I started working honestly and knew the difference between my earlier work and this job. Overall, it was a different experience. I got the best performer prize as well after two months for software testing.

It was obvious that my parents and family were happy that I had got a job again and it seemed to be to my liking.

Getting a job may be a simple thing for others, but it was a really big thing for me, to get my confidence back and to be happy as numerous things depended on it, including my dream of writing and my family's trust.

It was good to get an opportunity to work in a big brand MNC and start a fresh career in a pleasant work environment, and with a certain amount of flexibility. Most importantly, when people start appreciating you, you must feel a little confident and move ahead. My parents, family and friends were happy hearing this news. So I felt proud and satisfied and was happy I was changing myself. I cannot say much about the money I was earning because I had joined as a fresher, but the salary was good enough to survive in a city like Bangalore after sending some home. My passion for writing was also reignited and I got enough time to work on that over the weekends. Though I must admit I had learnt a lot while working in the telecom sector. It had taught me perseverance, patience and diligence.

I had dreamt of becoming an engineer and working in this kind of an environment when I was a child. The question is, is this the meaning of life? Should I forget my spirit? Should I live a normal life as other people do? Job, marriage, children, family and then, the end of life? Should there not be an aim to do something different? I have learnt something but also received something special from god and I will use this as a blessing. I will keep my dream alive. I received a lot of help from others while studying. I will try to help others if and when I am capable of doing so in the future.

Everyone has a dream during childhood and everyone has the right to fulfill it. If they need some help, then one should encourage and support them. There is love in this world which gives strength to fight difficult situations and fulfill dreams and I am really lucky I got this chance once. Thanks G! I can say positively this love gifted me many things in my life and I came out a better man.

♋

Generally it happens that when someone gets a smooth path in life, they ignore their dream and spirit. When things come easily to them, they think who cares? On the other hand, if you have too many problems and struggle too much in life, it is difficult to dream again. I had a strong desire to do something apart from my job. God also wanted me to keep my dream alive. That is why I believe that after a certain interval, I came face to face with G again in March, almost an year later. I was at the railway station to drop one of my friends. We wanted to get on the train and wish him good bye. I saw G standing near the gate on the train with her child on her lap. It seemed like she was waiting for me. She did not find any difficulty recognizing me, but I crossed her with my face averted. When I was returning, I saw her standing there with her daughter and her relatives. I could not resist giving her a glance and our eyes met. She had a little smile on her face. She thought I would say hello to her, but I passed by without saying anything.

Then, I heard her say, "Beta, say bye to your papa," while getting down the train. I thought her husband must be nearby and so moved away without looking back. I had struggled a lot to just see her in the past, and was not able to even see her during our school days. And here we were bumping into each other unexpectedly. Although this was how it was, throughout our lives, yet we kept getting chances to reconnect with each other. Maybe god wanted us to see each other from time to time and wanted to remind me of something until I got an answer!

I had lost that girl from my life, but had gained so many things in place of that and whatever the situation, love was always alive.

Who knows, if she had continued to be a part of my life, then, I may not have been able to learn so many things! The most important thing for a human is being a good person, knowing his duty, his value and to be true and pure in his views. Being true and good is a reward in itself.

I could have led a busy life simply spending my energy on my job, family and friends, but something deep inside me inspired me to share what I have done, what I wanted to do and other such little details of my life. It is a little hard for others to understand and that's why my friends always seem to have a feeling that I am an odd person! Sometimes they even wonder if something is wrong with me. But nothing is wrong. I just think I am a little crazy.

In our case, G is now married to someone else and even has a baby girl. Now that she is a mother, she will also know the extreme value of love. I understand that due to certain compulsions, women cannot freely decide what to do with their lives. But, she is happy and happiness is all I wish for her and her family. This story does not limit me to romance, but it is an inner voice that encourages me to value goodness and helps me connect to god. And, that for me is incredible strength.

Although G lives in Bangalore, she visits her parental home in Bihar regularly. It is just a few kilometres away from my parents' house, so we get some news of her family and how she and her family are doing. She comes with her child to visit her parents. She needs milk for her child. It is a bit difficult to get pure cow's milk, but my grandfather had a cowshed. So milk is supplied from my home for her child's need. In the Hindu tradition, the cow is also called Gau Mata, and is treated like a mother. This cow had grown up in my home and sometimes my mother had fed the calf grass with her own hands to help it grow well. I know how difficult it is to maintain a cow's calf and to help it grow. So milk was supplied for a kid by a mother with love and understanding of a mother for another mother.

I remembered how they had debated with each other when they used to meet each other in the temple, but now maternal love had brought them closer and my mother had helped in getting milk for G's child. A mother knows the real value of love for a child. I was surprised when I heard they even talk to each other happily now.

☙

Madhu and Tanya still talk to me. Tanya opted for her higher education in English literature from a reputed college in Indore. Soon I came to know Madhu was going to get married as her parents had wanted her to.

Tanya came to know that there was nothing between Madhu and me and Madhu was getting married to someone else. She too knew that it was hard for me to think of love and marriage at this point in my life as I had other ambitions to fulfill. After a few months, on Madhu's marriage day, I got a call from Tanya.

"You did not come to the wedding but at least wish her," she said.

I said, "Yeah, I remember. And it is impossible to forget you people." I asked her to hand over the phone to Madhu.

Madhu seemed excited, but asked me quite sadly, "Why didn't you come? Anyway, I can understand you are too far from us."

I sighed and said, "First of all, congratulations!! And, I'd already told you earlier I may not make it and I am so sorry for that. But my blessings will be with you always, stay happy and blessed."

She said, "Thank you and be in touch".

She handed over the phone to Tanya. I asked, taking a deep breath, "When is your turn, ma'am?"

She was a little emotional and said, "Madhu is going far from us, into a new family, she will forget us."

I said, "Do not worry… we will not let her escape from us. I will see you guys very soon. Will talk to you all soon. I must have told you about my book so please read it when it comes, you will come to know more about our past and our good times."

She assured me she would.

Small happiness can be forsaken if one has a big dream. I kept mine alive even after so many hurdles. It is very painful when I look back into my past and remember those difficult days – how hard I struggled to become a fighter and not give up on life. Time teaches lessons to everyone. There are no girls in my life after G, but the blessings of many different women gave strength and a different story to my life.

It is wonderfully exhilarating to fight for a dream. But, when someone puts a price on your dreams, the value of your soul and your spirit becomes zero. This happened to me too. Because there will always be people who won't quite understand your goals and will push you to value money more than anything else. It could be your family or your friends, telling you to find a position to earn more. But, just for their sake, your dream or happiness cannot be abandoned.

June 2012

Amar was now all grown up and fully involved in politics. I was not aware of his activities anymore and also what his relationship with G's family was like. Was he with G's father or against him, I did not know. But, I was still in touch with him and I told him about my intentions to write a book – an inspirational book that included my personal experiences as well as fictional work. He was excited to hear about this and wanted to know more. I asked him to wait until I had finished writing it. He was sure it was about G and was quite excited to see his name in the book as well. The news about the book reached G's father as well.

I did not know how he came to know about our past, and what exactly he had heard about us. He may have received some wrong information about my intentions as well. Because, when G's father heard about my book, he was a little tense and wanted to know what exactly I had written.

Next morning when I returned a call to a missed call from unknown number, it turned out to be G's father. First he introduced himself as we had interacted once or twice in my childhood. He asked me instinctively, "How are you?"

"Namsate Uncle, good, I am good. How are you? How do you remember me?" I was a little worried.

After a pause asked further, "I heard you are writing a book. What kind of book is that?" His voice fell on my eardrums like Amrish Puri's.

I wondered who had told him about it, but after controlling myself, I said in an unsteady voice, "Yes Uncle, but this is a very simple story of my life. A memoir with fiction as well."

He said, "Good, I can understand and if something wrong was done to you by our family in the past, I am sorry."

I paused and said, "No no, Uncle it is okay, you please do not worry. My writing has nothing to do with any other person. It is simply about my struggle which I have moulded into a story."

Then I asked courageously, "How did you come to know about my story, Uncle? Was it Amar who told you?"

He said, "Yes, he is here… you can talk to him as well."

He handed over the phone to Amar. I asked Amar freely, "Hey, what did you tell him about my writing and about our past?"

He said, "Nothing, just spoke a little about your past and G's friendship with you and wondered if you'll write something amazing about us."

I said making a joke, "No, Amar, I am not writing to target someone, or one's family, it is about a wish, a dream to write something which motivates me."

Then I continued, "I will talk to you later in detail as you are my friend and you can understand. For now, please assure G's father there is nothing to worry about."

He said, "Okay, you also do not worry."

I asked him to hand over the phone to G's father again and said, "Sorry for any misunderstanding, Uncle. Please do not worry."

He understood, said, "Okay, take care, bye."

G's father must have informed his daughter about this before talking to me. This must have bothered G as well because before long I got a call from her too.

Another call from an unknown number. I heard a woman's voice saying, "How are you?"

I thought for a few moments and realized it was G. "I am good, how about you? How did you get my number?"

She said, "I am also fine, it's been a long time." She paused for some time and asked, "How is your life and work? I heard you have written a book. What is this book about?"

I asked, "Who told you?"

"My dad told me and he asked me what our relationship was. Have you written something about us?"

I said laughing, "Oh god, why is he so serious? And you as well please note it is not about anyone, nor have I written anything wrong about others. It is about my creative work. Just for my understanding, I have simply followed my heart. I thought I should do it for myself, to be happy."

She said softly, "I can understand you."

I said instinctively, "I can assure you nothing is written which will hurt you or your family. It is just a good thing for me. I have followed my heart, so please let me do this because I have struggled a lot for this."

I wished her to be happy, but now she was emotional and said, "I wanted to see you again but did not get chance to even say I was going to get married. That Diwali when you met with an accident during your college days, I wanted to tell you about it and at the same time I wanted to know your opinion. But you were not well and I didn't want to stress you. And before I knew it, I was married..."

I sighed and said, "No worries, there is no point going back to the past now. We are all well and happy, so let's be happy without any complaint or misunderstandings."

I added, "You are happy, that is fine. I do not have any complaints about anyone now, and I am happy too."

She asked mumbling, "You are not married yet, when will you marry?"

I asked, jokingly, "Marry? Whom? You?"

She laughed aloud and said, "So funny... you will marry me? A married girl? *Shaadi shuda ladaki se shaadi karoge, haan?*"

I smiled, and asked, "So you think you are still a girl?"

She laughed and said, "Yeah, I am."

I said, "Oh! I thought you are an old lady now. How is your girl?" I asked.

She said, "She is doing good and tells me things like '*In kapdo me main moti lagoongi tumahri tarah* [In these clothes, I'll look fat like you.] She is only four years old."

And we laughed about it together. I knew she had not wanted to tell her family about her feelings for me. Her father was not as angry as she had feared, but I guess she thought, why bother her family about her wishes. What if they don't react well. Anyway, there is no point in feeling sad about the past now. What she thought at that time... only she knows.

She asked me about my marriage again and I told her, I was happy as I was for the moment. I was enjoying other things in life and sometimes, it is hard to learn in a crowd what you would be able to learn when alone.

Then I said, "By the way, your daughter is so cute."

And she asked, "*Aur mein?*"

I said, "You can get an answer from your husband." We laughed.

She went back to my book. "You struggled a lot. What I can tell you is that your story is worth telling and wish you all the best! It's been a long struggle and it happened because of me. I am sorry."

She sighed and said, "I will read your book for sure."

I said "Not to worry! Thank you and you take care of yourself and your family."

I tried to lighten the moment by singing a song from Veer-Zaara,

> "*Do pal ruka khwabon ka karvaan, aur fir chal diye tum kahan hum kahan ....*
>
> *Do pal ki thi ye dilon ki dastan, aur fir chal diye tum kahan hum kahan ..."*

She was about to start sobbing but I laughed ignoring her trembling voice and said, "That is all about my story."

She said controlling herself, "Good luck!"

She did not tell me clearly about how she feels about her present life. It is true – love remains forever, just gets transferred from one energy to another like the rules of conservation of energy. If it is pure, it may not remain as a relationship, but also as good impressions!

There is still a fire inside my veins which always explodes in my blood to alert me about my goal. Thanks to G, she finally admitted that my story is worth telling.

Expectations hurt more sometimes, but on the other side, faith pays the value for the same. I expected more from my life, but it took too long for me to find the real me. Moreover, life is all about experiences, either good or bad. No matter what my experiences were, each one had an impact on my life. It was all about how I perceived my journey through life since childhood. My attitude was sometimes negative, sometimes positive, but at some point, I realized that there was no meaning in hanging on to negative attitudes. It only leads to weakness and dwelling over loss and pain.

Whatever we can achieve will be through positive thinking and self-encouragement. I had to seek encouragement in small events, simple pleasures, beauty of nature and also accept that god is ever present behind all his creations. And, I think belief in god makes all the difference in your life as it helps you believe in yourself.

We all dream during our childhood, but in the journey of life, sometimes these dreams get blurred knowingly or unknowingly. Problems are part and parcel of life. No matter what kind they are or when and how they will come, but our attitude towards them makes the difference. We need to be ready to face them. More importantly, we learn a lesson from each and every problem.

To be an engineer was my childhood dream. I wanted to do my engineering from a top national level college like an IIT, get a dream job and respect in society. But life had something else in store for me. I made myself strong and thought I will fight against my weaknesses. It worked and every event and person seemed to be quite positive. It was like god was directing me in this manner. Thank you friends for being so supportive every time I needed help from you.

Tanya tried her best to edit the story as she is a professional editor in a reputed publishing firm and helped me find a suitable way to get this book out.

It was good to see Asha after ten long years. She was amazed to see the changes in me and wished me luck.

☞

I accepted that I was responsible for whatever happened to me in my life. I struggled through my first job for survival, even though it was not in my best interests. I slowly learned to judge for myself, to recognize what I need and to work on getting it. Somewhere along this journey, I created a new aim and a new identity for myself. This became as important as my childhood dream of becoming an IITian.

As for love, the real meaning of love I experienced is not simply falling in love with someone. It is also about how happy you are in different circumstances and conditions, it is about sharing sadness, happiness and experiences with others, and it is about sharing love and laughter with people around you. It is not about fear and weakness; it is all about how much someone loves you and if you love them enough to get into a relationship again! And if you are disappointed in love…

Fall in love again. Life is a journey of new experiences!